Even when the stones yell out,
I'll never hear their cry.
Unbalanced, petrified, I shout;
Unsilenced, screaming, 'WHY?'

Fin Rackman (The Stone Balancer)

The Stone Balancer
by John Townsend

Published by Raven Books
An imprint of Ransom Publishing Ltd.
Unit 7, Brocklands Farm, West Meon, Hampshire GU32 1JN, UK
www.ransom.co.uk

ISBN 978 178591 362 4
First published in 2017

Printed and bound in Great Britain by Clays Ltd, St Ives plc

A CIP catalogue record of this book is available from the British Library.

THE STONE BALANCER

John Townsend

August. Sunday. Sunset. Warm sea breezes.
Lapping waves on shingle.
Seafront crowds. Bustling cafés and bars.
Live music. Wafts of vinegary fish and chips.
Dark beaches. Darkening sky. Darker cliffs.
A cry of gulls. A dying scream. Eerie silence.

Midnight. Moonlight.
Moving shadows on a cliff.
The strike of a match. The curl of a flame.
The flare of frantic fire.
Sparks in surreptitious eyes at sea
… secretly drifting in on the forbidden tide.

Breaking the Silence

I didn't hear a siren when the police car skidded to a halt at the quayside after midnight. Its flashing lights swirled around the harbour, sparking across dark water and sweeping over moored yachts swaying like ocean phantoms in the mist. Beach huts shone in bursts of shuddering blue, shimmering in a pulsing ghostly glow. The silence tightened – stifling my thumping heart and the frantic pounding in my head.

They bundled me into the back of the car. Police jumped in beside me, wrenching a seatbelt round my waist. As we sped off in a spray of shingle, I looked back at the moonlit beach disappearing behind us and I knew it was over. At least, the first part was over … and I was relieved.

Endings can be so uncertain. They might be new beginnings in disguise. There's no question about the first beginning – ten days before my fourteenth birthday. Even though it was back in August, it's taken ages to write everything down; beginning, middle and sort-of end – the complete mystery. Maybe now someone will believe the 'silent witness' and understand my words, balancing them with hard facts like solid stones – from mysterious beginnings to uncertain endings; of the grim discovery from my fourteenth summer.

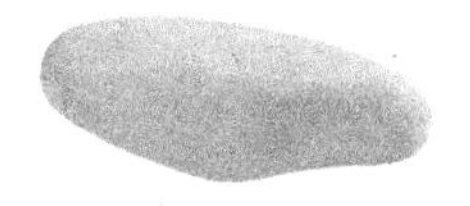

ONE

Monday 15th August

I was dreaming of Grandad again – just like when he died after Christmas.

Struggling from sleep, I sat up and saw him at the foot of my bed, pointing at the old wardrobe. 'Don't forget it's in there,' he smiled. 'I bought that wardrobe with my first wages, so it's a bit special. Just like you are to me, Fin. I used to hide all sorts from your gran in that little cubbyhole underneath. She never knew it was there. I want you to keep that biscuit tin safe inside till you grow up … and never let *you know who* find it. Don't even tell your mum. It's our special secret, Fin. You and me – the best of pals – the two wise monkeys.'

He gave a wheezy chuckle and turned away.

'Please come back, Grandad.' I tried to call after him, but my words made no sound. I could only mouth silently, 'I want you to stay forever.'

But I knew that would never happen.

I woke up late, after sleeping through two alarm clocks – one under my pillow that vibrates like mad and the other that fires a spinning missile that's meant to make you jump out of bed. They both failed to wake me, so it was just before eleven o'clock when, all bleary-eyed, I pulled back the curtains to see brilliant sunlight sparkling on the sea. A great day for the beach.

Usually Mum woke me before she went to work, but I guessed she'd overslept, too. I decided to make her a mug of tea, grab some toast then head off on my bike.

I've got to be honest, the stone-balancing craze was becoming a bit of an obsession. It's one of those things that seems to take you over. It's magic when you find just the right shape and size of rocks that can pile up at weird angles and make it look like you've had to use superglue rather than masses of patience and practice to sense how to keep them all in place. I love the concentration it takes to work out the centre of gravity of each stone.

Some of my masterpieces up to ten rocks high can last for days above the high-tide mark, if it's not too windy or kids don't lob pebbles at them. A few of the designs an old man does on that same beach are totally awesome – like amazing sculptures and works of art. He seems to go into a trance and talks about finding a point of silence inside himself. I guess I should be able to do that, but I just place one stone on top of another and hope for the best. Inner silence like that isn't really my thing. My silence is different.

I had to shake Mum to wake her up. 'I've got you some tea, Mum. It's late.'

She went into one of her panics. 'Has work called? I'm supposed to be there by now.'

'It's no use asking me,' I said. 'I've only just got up myself. Try your answerphone.'

She grabbed my arm. 'Fin, look at me. Make sure you take your phone if you go out today. Don't go in the sea and be careful near the rocks. Send me a text to tell me what you're doing and where you are. Keep to the quiet roads – I worry about you on your bike. They said on the news a boy in London had headphones on, so didn't hear a lorry behind him and got knocked off his bike. You must take care, Fin.'

'I haven't got headphones and I don't do music,' I snapped back.

'You know exactly what I mean, Fin. Sometimes you don't realise ... Take some food and a drink from the fridge. I won't be going to work now but I might have to go out. I'll text you to let you know when I'm coming back.'

She didn't let go of my arm until I said about three times that I understood her every word.

I left her in bed, put on my backpack, ran to the shed to get my bike and headed off to the cliff road. The heat bounced off the tarmac as it rushed beneath my wheels and I had that tingling feeling of excitement in my arms and legs as the sun beat down on my body and the warm breeze flapped through my T-shirt.

It was great to be out, with no one to boss me or fuss and I could be free all day. I've always loved going down to the beach below the cliffs in the next bay from our bungalow, as not many people know the way down and they can't get round the headland at high tide. Few people from the caravan park behind the hedge that I whizzed past seemed to use the cliff path below their field – where smoke was wafting from what I assumed were lazy breakfast barbecues.

As soon as I smelt the seaweed, felt the sea breeze on my face and saw the sunlight swirling on the water, I couldn't wait to get down there on the sand. On windy days, long before I'd clamber down and see the massive waves, it was awesome to feel the spray on my skin, breathe in the salty blasts and sense the thundering thuds shuddering through the rocks. The seagulls get flung around all over the place but they don't seem that bothered. They just flap a bit, ride the gusts and carry on doing their own thing. I like to think I'm a bit like that. Maybe I was a seagull in a previous life. Maybe that's why I tried to glide through the storm that blew into my world that summer.

I left my bike under a gorse bush on the cliff edge, then scrambled down a steep winding path, overgrown in places by brambles and bracken. My trainers slipped in the dust so, to stop me careering down out of control, I had to grab tough clumps of long grass that cut my fingers. Each time I skidded, trickles of stones spilled down the cliff in a mini-avalanche onto the rocks below. About halfway down, at a slippery corner of a zigzag, my feet slid from under me and I hurtled off the path into the undergrowth, grabbing at anything that could stop me nose-diving out of control. Brambles tore at my hands and, as I sprawled into a clump of nettles, I saw a woman's pale pink sandal, speckled with dried blood, caught on a twig. Just then a man in scuffed boots with odd laces, muddy grey jogging bottoms, red binoculars strapped round his neck and dragging a windbreak rolled round a spade jogged up the path. He spat as he lumbered past.

As I hadn't heard him, I was really startled at his sudden appearance, but even more shocked that he spat right at me, leaving me to tumble down and head-butt a gorse bush. He was gone as soon as he'd appeared – in a flash. I didn't see his face – just the back of his head, a sweaty brown T-shirt caked in sand, and a tattooed left arm. And that was it, he'd gone. But his image didn't leave me; a big, stocky bulk of a man – the last image I saw of him, as I dragged myself back to the path. Blood was smeared on one knee of his jogging bottoms, so maybe he was rushing to get medical help. Even so, that spit seemed perfectly aimed at me.

Wiping my cuts and stings, as well as the man's gob of frothy saliva sliding down my shoulder, I groped my way back towards the path. It was then my hand touched something smooth under a clump of heather and I pulled out a small purple wallet. It was new, open and seemed to be empty, but I took it with me as I headed on down. I zipped the wallet safely in a pocket on my backpack, intending to check for a name and address later. Right then I just wanted to be down on the beach where I could now see the tide was halfway out and the sand was still damp and shiny.

I ran down to the breaking waves near to where a woman was paddling and throwing a stick into the water for her dog to fetch. Further up the beach a man with a metal detector swept the foot of the cliffs, picking through dried seaweed. Children at the far end played with a Frisbee, their wet hair and discarded towels showing they'd already been swimming. Otherwise, the beach was empty and I had the freshly-washed stones to myself, far away from anyone else.

After gathering a mix of boulders, smaller rocks of different colours and all sorts of smoothed stones, I began building by balancing one on top of the other or at a slight angle to the one below. The art is to make each stone appear to defy gravity or seem too big to balance on the one beneath it. I was soon totally absorbed in constructing little towers that stood firmly without swaying. If each stone is balanced carefully enough, the sculpture won't collapse – but if it does, you just start again without getting flustered. The secret is to keep calm, still and really relaxed. I don't often do 'relaxed' so maybe it's a Virgo thing that drives me to get something just right without anyone able to criticise. It can be a struggle being a perfectionist in an imperfect world, so I love to get lost in my own head without worrying about time.

Eventually my efforts began to pay off as, after however long it took, I'd finished a spectacular circle of stone towers that people on the beach came to admire and take selfies beside. It was only when I took pictures myself on my phone that I saw a text from Mum.

Fin, need to talk. Please come home. Sorry.

I texted back, sending a picture.

Look, I'm a genius. See you soon.

I didn't hurry back. I knew we'd argue. I was so fed up with Mum fussing all the time. 'Be careful. Don't go far. Keep in contact.' All my life I feel I've been held back. Grandad never stopped me doing stuff and always encouraged me to take risks, but since he died I've felt I was back in a cage.

I was sure, as I cycled home, that Mum would be in a mood and it would spoil everything. We'd probably have another row. But I had no idea, when I entered the kitchen with, 'Hi, I'm back,' that I was about to face more than I expected.

'It looks like you need a bath,' Mum said as soon as I walked in. 'Look at the state of you. You've caught the sun – I hope you put some cream on. I bet you haven't drunk enough – it's easy to dehydrate in this heat, you know.'

'I'm fine,' I said, turning away to avoid a torrent of further nags and to stop myself screaming. In fact, I sometimes think I should add an '*e*' on the end of my name and have 'I'm Fine' tattooed on my forehead. Anything to stop fuss.

'I wish you wouldn't spend so much time on your own, Fin,' she continued. It was like the same old record playing over and over again. 'Why don't you bring a friend home or mix a bit more?'

'You know I like being by myself.'

She sighed and looked like she had all the troubles of the world on her shoulders. 'I guess it's my fault for letting you spend all your time with Grandad rather than with kids your own age. Sometimes you even sound like him – more like a quaint old man than a ... '

'A gobby yob?' I laughed. 'Just you wait till my birthday – then you'll notice the difference. I'll turn into a stroppy chav then, so watch out.'

She gave me one of her funny looks, so I gave my cheekiest grin back and said, 'It's not my fault you gave birth to me at the end of August.'

I don't believe in all that horoscope stuff, but I showed her what it said in one of her magazines: *Virgos are undemonstrative and introvert, often being loners with waters that run deep. Wise, witty and watchful for detail, the Virgo is sensitive, has a good understanding of human nature and can effectively help people solve their problems.*

'So that's what I am, Mum – just get over it!'

Instead of her giggling or chasing me down the garden waving a broom for a laugh, as she sometimes did, she took me by surprise. She went very serioius and said, 'Let's hope you can help me solve one of my problems, Fin.'

She rolled up her sleeve to show the bruises up her arm; black, blue and purple. Even yellow. Everywhere.

'Who's done that to you?' I asked. 'Whatever happened?' For a horrible moment I thought Uncle Calvin had come back.

'It was the shed door knocking into me in the wind. The doctor sent me for tests. It's something to do with dodgy blood, apparently. It might explain all my nosebleeds and headaches as well.'

I told her not to worry, but I knew that was a waste of time. Mum could win a gold medal for worrying. She was always worried about something – usually in case she was made redundant from her job at the Tourist Information Centre in town, even though the place is heaving with tourists all year.

She held my face in her hands and sighed, 'I worry what's to become of you, Fin. It's a tough old world out there, eh?'

I told her she didn't have to worry about me any more, but she turned away and mumbled something which I didn't catch – but I guessed. I knew she was about to cry again.

I've always been used to Mum crying. This time it was about her feeling guilty for not taking me away on holiday. 'I'm so sorry, Fin. I really need a holiday, what with being so tired all the time – but I just can't afford it at the moment. When they sell Grandad's flat I promise I'll take you somewhere amazing. That's if Uncle Calvin doesn't take it all.'

I didn't say anything. I just remembered what Grandad had told me just before he died, so I shrugged and went to my room. I sat on the end of my bed and stared at the wardrobe – and at my face in the mirror on the door. It always reassured me that I could see a bit of Grandad in the shape of my face, but I dreaded ever looking like Uncle Calvin, with his puffy double-chin. Even so, maybe I shared some of his naffest genes. What a pity you can't get a gene transplant or get to choose your own relatives, I thought.

It was then I saw my face morph into Grandad's in the mirror. There was no sound, but I knew what the lips were saying. 'Take a look in the wardrobe, Fin. Make sure the tin is safely hidden inside. Remember everything I told you. Guard it with your life.'

TWO

The wardrobe's wooden floor lifted to reveal a dark space underneath. It was where Grandad's biscuit tin had remained hidden since the very last time I saw him. That was on Christmas Day, when he was in a wheelchair and so ill, but he'd insisted on spending 'quality time in private with my best friend and grandson'. It wasn't totally private because Maisie, his guide dog, lay at his feet by the wardrobe while he told me everything. He winked and said she was one hundred percent trustworthy and wouldn't breathe a word to anyone.

'That tin has all sorts in it; various bits and bobs, family heirlooms and a few papers. Keep them under wraps. When you're eighteen you can decide what to do with them and show Mum then if you want. But it's best if your Uncle Calvin never gets his grubby paws on them.

The thing is, Fin – you know I think the world of you. You've been more than my eyes these last years. Maisie loves you, too … ' She looked up at me with perfect timing, with those big brown Labrador eyes. I stroked her head as Grandad asked me a question that took me by surprise.

'What did you think of Uncle Calvin when you saw him on my birthday?' His blind eyes opened wide as he waited for me to reply.

'If I'm honest, we didn't speak to each other. I still don't really like him, Grandad. I know I shouldn't say that, but he doesn't like me either. Nor does Jasmine.'

'Well, they certainly don't think much of me. Once I've gone, they'll be crawling over everything in my flat, trying to get their claws on my money. I don't want to tell your mum what he's really like, as she's already got enough on her plate. But I'll warn you, Fin. Never trust Calvin. He's got a nasty side that your mum doesn't know about – because Gran and I kept it all quiet for years. As far as Mum knows, Calvin went off to university, then backpacking around Australia.'

'I know,' I said. 'She's told me about it.'

'But that's the point,' Grandad shook his head sadly. 'He did neither.'

I was concentrating hard, watching Grandad's face very closely and hanging on his every word as he added slowly, 'He was in prison for three years.'

I said nothing as I tried to imagine the uncle I didn't see very often as a convict behind bars. I was stunned, but as the news sank in, part of me wasn't too surprised.

'He broke his mother's heart. Mine too, for that matter. When he moved away from home he got in a bad crowd, got mixed up in all sorts of trouble and went off the rails. He's been a ne'er-do-well ever since. I always reckoned drugs did something to his mind. He was convicted for assault and diagnosed with something called IED; intermittent explosive disorder. That's basically a terrible temper, but he's calmed down since then. We didn't dare tell your mum about it all as she was going through a hard time herself. You know how stressed she can get. We were going to tell her everything in time, but then her world fell apart and I couldn't knock her confidence when she was at rock bottom.'

I knew exactly what he was talking about. 'You mean ten years ago, when I was three?' I asked.

He nodded. 'When you got very ill and we nearly lost you.' His eyes filled as he turned to tell Maisie. 'The doctors said little Fin wouldn't make it. It was the last straw. That's when Fin's dad walked out. It was all too much.'

'Mum never talks about all that,' I butted in. 'She told me once that my dad was from another planet and, for all she knew, he now lived on the moon. Even now I stare from my bedroom window at the full moon when it hangs in the midnight sky and turns the sea gold. That's always so awesome to watch, but I still stick up two fingers – as it reminds me of a dad who disappeared without trace one morning when I was three and a half.'

Grandad reached out to touch me. His hand was unusually shaky, cold and bony.

'Fin, you're a miracle and I love the way you talk to me. Back then was a bad time and I blame all that for bringing on Gran's heart trouble. It was a terrible shock for your mum to find her dead in this very room. That's why I've tried to protect Mum ever since. Not that I need to worry now as you're doing her the power of good. Even so ... ' he leaned forward and tapped his nose, 'best not tell her about her brother, eh? Just be on your guard but hush-hush. Let sleeping dogs lie, I reckon. Isn't that so, Maisie?' He smiled as he patted her and she rolled on her side.

That was my last memory of the man I adored.

I opened the wardrobe door as I relived that conversation from nearly eight months before. Lifting the false floor, I peered in at the biscuit tin hidden inside. I hadn't opened it since I'd put my letter in there after Grandad's funeral. Somehow I'd hoped he might be able to see again and read what I'd written. The envelope was exactly as I'd left it with two words written on it:

To Grandad.

Although I remembered most of what I'd written, I took out the letter and read every word of my best handwriting once more.

Dear Grandad,

My teacher said it might help if I write to you and let you know how I feel. She's noticed a change in me, as I'm'not like my old self'. Surprise, surprise! She's the teacher I told you about. Mrs Holmes is brilliant – the one who told me I was as bright as a button but added with a laugh 'despite everything'. The bad news is she's retiring in the summer at the end of my Year 9. That's another blow as she's got me reading and helps me with dyslexia and stuff.

There were loads of people at your funeral and they all said amazing things. I didn't cry till afterwards. Even Uncle Calvin did a good talk and he really impressed Mum. Jasmine drank too much and slept in the car most of the day, but even she scrubbed up well for a 'large Goth with big issues'. You used to laugh at how I described her and everything else to you. I so miss all that. I also miss Maisie and I hope we did the right thing. Mum and I so wanted to keep her ourselves, but after a long talk we decided we should let her go to another blind person as she's still young and such a brilliant working dog. We thought that's what you'd want, but it meant we'd never be able to see her again. That hurt so much.

When the van came to collect Maisie, Mum and I locked ourselves in the shed and blubbed like babies all afternoon, before going wild at the theme park and going on every single ride. We screamed till we were totally pooped, then had hot dogs, ice cream and candyfloss before going for a massive curry. Weirdly, we weren't sick, even when we drank bottles of coke watching a spooky late night foreign film with subtitles. I bet you'd have been real chuffed with us. We didn't tell Uncle Calvin.

I miss Maisie so much – but not as much as I miss you. To be honest, I don't think I'll ever be the same again. This year hasn't been that great so far and I reckon it's the end of the Fin you knew. Or as they'd say in France, 'le fin de Fin'.

Thanks for being so epic, Grandad – and my inspiration forever.

As soon as I returned the tin to its hiding place in the wardrobe, I saw Mum's face in the mirror beside me. Spinning round, I just hoped she hadn't seen Grandad's secret tin, but I soon knew she was in manic mode and unaware of anything – apart from whatever was on her mind. She sat on the bed and told me to sit beside her, making sure I was looking at her face. 'I need to talk to you, Fin. I'm sorry I haven't cooked anything. I'll get something from the freezer or open a tin. I haven't had time, what with everything else.'

'What did you think of my photo?' I asked. 'I did some great stone-balancing today.' I could usually calm things a bit by changing the subject.

'Very nice, love. I just wish you'd do it with a few friends. Mix a bit, that's all.'

'I'm going to print off that picture and make some cards. I might sell a few,' I said, ignoring her.

'That's not a bad idea,' she answered, although she was obviously thinking about something else. 'I could sell them at the Tourist Office if you like.'

'Sweet!' I grinned. 'I'd like to make a few quid for the

Guide Dogs. Grandad would want that. It could be our little business in memory of him.'

'The only thing is, I might be off work for a while,' she went on, biting her lip.

'It looks like I'll need to go into hospital soon, love.' She looked away but I saw tears drip on the duvet. 'I didn't tell you everything earlier – about what the doctor said. You don't need to know all the details, but I've got blood problems and may need some treatment. I'm afraid it looks like you may have to go and stay with Uncle Calvin for a little while.'

'I'm going to print my pictures,' I said, without looking at her. I went to my printer, leaving her sitting there talking at me non-stop, although I had no idea what she was going on about. I didn't want to think about what she was saying. Eventually she left me alone, although I didn't see her go.

As I was doing stuff on my laptop and choosing images to print while trying not to dwell on what Mum had said, she sent me an email.

> Sorry, Fin. I didn't know how to tell you. I've got something called MDS. It's best if you Google it so you know what it means. Please don't worry. That's my job! Love Mum.

Knowing how she always feared the worst and worried whatever, I did as she said and tapped in MDS, expecting to see something like Mild Depression Symptoms. I guessed it was probably just one of those 'midlife things' that a few tablets could sort out. But a long word that I couldn't say came up: Myelodysplasia. I read some of the description but didn't take it all in.

> In MDS, your bone marrow doesn't make enough healthy red blood cells, white blood cells and/or platelets. Instead, it makes abnormal cells that are not fully developed. Treatment will depend on your type of MDS and your level of risk. The aim is to get the blood cells in your bloodstream back to normal, and manage symptoms. If your MDS has only a low risk of turning into cancer, you may not need any treatment at first, just regular blood tests.

The word 'cancer' screamed in my head and burst through my silence like a juggernaut. I swore and threw myself on my bed. Why did this have to come crashing into our lives right now? All I ever wanted was to be left alone and to get away from all the constant fussing from adults – and now cancer was muscling in as well. I'd already seen what that did to Grandad. Although I knew I could do nothing about that scary intruder, I would certainly do everything in my power to stop the other – Uncle Calvin. The last thing we needed was him on the scene – or me on his.

I vowed right then I would take control and do something drastic. Nothing was going to make me live with him and his gross partner.

'I know it's not easy for you, Fin,' Mum said later, over a plate of spaghetti hoops on toast. 'But it's not easy for me at the moment, either. I should feel a bit livelier at the weekend when I've had another blood transfusion, so maybe we can go out somewhere then. Have a think where you'd like to go. We'll have a bit of fun, eh? We may not have a chance again this holiday if I need to have chemo.'

'I'm not going to Uncle Calvin's, Mum. Grandad once told me ... ' I stopped myself just in time. 'He told me Uncle Calvin doesn't really understand me. We might not get on and you wouldn't want that, would you?'

She was about to argue, but I stroked her hand and she smiled. 'We'll see, love. I'll do the best I can for you, but I haven't got any answers right now. We've got a lot of thinking to do, but like the specialist said, "One step at a time". He's arranged for me to visit someone who's already gone through the treatment, so I'm going there tomorrow. It's another day off work, but I'm sure they'll understand. I can't face going in to tell them yet, so can I ask a big favour, Fin?'

'Let me guess,' I said, trying to sound as cheery as I could. 'You either want me to dress up as the town crier and make an announcement outside the Tourist Office, or you want me to pop in and give them a note.'

She came over and gave me a hug and this time it was me who fought back the tears. 'Fin,' she said calmly, 'I'd be so lost without you, love. I really mean it. You mean the absolute world to me.'

That night I couldn't sleep. I lay with the curtains open to let the moonlight spill into my room. In the wardrobe mirror at the foot of my bed, I watched the moon slowly move across the sky and brush the sea with specs of gold. It should have seemed magical, but I couldn't help sticking up two fingers to curse the moon and the growing shadows looming in the darkness.

THREE

For a few seconds I was convinced a golden Labrador sitting in a bus shelter on the seafront was Maisie. She looked up at me and wagged her tail as I walked past, so I couldn't resist going over to talk to her. Her owner was a woman in dark glasses, but she wasn't blind and up close the dog didn't have Maisie's distinct little frown. I said something about Grandad but the woman didn't smile and I had no idea what she mumbled back, so I quickly headed off to the Tourist Office, clutching my bag of newly-printed cards.

As I walked up to the counter, I gave a quick wave to Sandra, Mum's boss. She looked at me nervously, as if I was about to take a sawn-off shotgun from my bag and demand all the carnival programmes. For some reason she always spoke to me as if I was three and a half – and a total moron. She pronounced every word really slowly with exaggerated mouth movements, like I was some kind of dumb puppy.

'Hello, Finley. Is Mum any better?'

'Not really,' I answered. 'She's got another appointment today and asked me to give you this note. I've also got some cards that she says you could sell for me – to make some money for charity.' I spoke quickly, hoping she would realise I wasn't the dimwit she thought I was. It made no difference.

'Ooh, they look lovely, sweetheart. Did you do all those yourself? What a clever boy. Hey, Marjorie, come over here and see what Finley has made. I'm going to buy a few myself to start the ball rolling.' She emptied coins from her purse onto the counter and when Marjorie came over, she whispered an aside that she seemed to think I wouldn't notice. 'It's Finley, Ali's boy. You know, the one I told you about. He's selling cards, bless him.'

Marjorie peered over the counter at me with a startled stare, as if she was expecting to discover a puff adder coiled on the carpet tiles. 'Well he looks just like his mum, doesn't he? It's amazing what those kids can do these days, isn't it? Schools can work wonders. Those cards look super, although I'm never really sure why people glue stones together on a pile.'

Although she was talking *at* me rather than *to* me, I said, 'It's called stone-balancing. Bit of a clue in the name. No glue was harmed in the building of my artistic creations.'

She stared at me with a nervy twitch, as if she hadn't

expected me to understand a word. 'I'll get you some coins from my bag,' she said, and went to the back of the office, followed by Sandra who mouthed to her in a stage whisper, assuming I couldn't tell what she was saying, 'It can't be easy for Ali bringing him up by herself, what with everything. It must be a trial.'

She returned and gave me a handful of coins. 'Take this money for now, Finley, and we'll try and sell the rest for you. Haven't you been a busy boy?'

'Yes,' I smiled, 'particularly as I'm still being house-trained.'

I left them to their stunned and silent stares.

I now had about ten pounds in loose change that I wanted to give to Guide Dogs, so I set off up the street to find the house I'd seen with a life-size guide dog statue outside, with a collecting box round its neck. About halfway along Braxted Avenue, past all the guest houses, I spotted the retro-looking statue outside number 21. Behind the gates a driveway led to black garage doors beside the front porch of an old-fashioned 1930s-style house with big bay windows and closed curtains.

Leaning my bike against the gates, I took a handful of coins from my pocket and began feeding them into the slot in the guide dog's collecting box. I was concentrating on pushing down coin after coin and counting how much was going in, so I didn't notice a little old woman in a wrap-over overall bustling down the drive towards me, waving a tea towel.

'Stop that. Stop that immediately. I've told you children before, it's not a toy. I can hear that bell indoors, you know. You just like to hear it ring each time you poke something in there, don't you? I soon know when you silly boys push stones and lolly sticks in. You mustn't do it as it clogs things up and takes forever to clean it out. You'll stop money going through, which we need for the guide dogs. Now off you go and don't do it again.'

I looked up at her, thinking, *well that's the thanks I get for trying to be helpful,* but I said with my saddest spaniel eyes, 'But it's my money I'm putting in – just over ten pounds. I've been raising money for you.'

The woman paused and looked me up and down. 'Really? Are you serious?'

'Yes. My Grandad had a guide dog and I want to help buy one for someone else.' I let my bottom lip wobble a bit to show I was upset.

'My dear, I'm so sorry. I thought you were one of those horrible little boys from the next street. I can't tell you how sorry I am. You must come in for a drink and a biscuit. I've got some puppies indoors if you'd like to see them.'

She opened the gate, ushered me through and up the steps into the porch, where the smell of cooking fish spilled from the hallway. 'I'm just boiling up off-cuts for the cats,' she said. 'I've got about twenty at the moment – and a few litters of kittens. We have an RSPCA cattery in the garage. I run a couple of animal charities here and we've always got a few stray pets to look after, as well as the odd injured seagull. Nothing is ever turned away. Now, come inside and tell me how you raised the money. We like to know who our friends are. You'd be surprised at how many enemies we have as well. Some people can be very cruel to animals, so we do all we can to stop them.'

She took me into a dark sitting room which had its own distinct animal smell, with each chair occupied by a sleeping cat. 'Sit down, dear,' she went on. 'Push Sooty off the armchair and make yourself comfy. I'm Mrs Boughtwood – what's your name?'

'Fin. Finley Rackman. I think my grandad knew you. He was Gerald Gibson.'

'Good heavens, I knew your grandfather for years. You look so much like him – the same mouth and chin. Lovely man. He often sent us funds, God bless him. Then it's a pleasure to meet you, Finley. I've got some chocolate cake in the kitchen – you must have some – nice thick icing on top. Sophie loves it. That's her practising the piano in the other room. Do you play?'

'Sorry? Play what?' I have to say, it was a struggle to keep up with all her gabbling. Her mind seemed to be darting from one thing to the next and I was still trying to work out what was moving in a closed cat basket on a wheelchair in the corner.

'The piano, dear. That's a rabbit in the basket. It's got an injured back and just came back from the vet. He was found in a ditch – the rabbit, not the vet. That's Sophie's wheelchair. She's on crutches, you see, but loves coming here for the animals and the piano. Would you like tea or a cold drink?'

My mind was spinning. 'Who's Sophie?'

She gave a sickly smile as if I was asking a stupid question and should have known the answer. 'Our granddaughter, dear.'

The name suddenly clicked in my head. 'I know Sophie Boughtwood. She's in the year above me at Community College. I've seen her in Mrs Holmes' room.'

Right on cue, Sophie appeared in the doorway. 'Hey, you're Fin,' she beamed. 'I've seen you around school. You're one of Mrs Holmes' cool kids – hashtag cute! I'm *so* going to miss her, aren't you? What are you doing here, anyway?'

'Your grandma dragged me in off the street,' I laughed.

'I thought Finley was a hooligan, Sophie. I was mistaken, of course.'

'You should've gone to Specsavers,' Sophie giggled.

'Enough of all that,' her Gran said, waving a tea towel. 'It's time for tea and cake. You two have a chat while I put the kettle on. What did you think of Sophie's playing, Finley? We're very proud of her.'

Before I could answer, Sophie was whispering in her gran's ear, so I just mumbled something about how I didn't really have much time for pianos.

Mrs Boughtwood stared at me for a few seconds, gave another of her sickly smiles, told Sophie to 'turf Rusty off the sofa and make yourselves comfy' and bustled from the room – leaving the two of us smiling at each other awkwardly.

'Gran is a bit eccentric, I'm afraid. She's really my

step-gran, but she's got a heart of gold and cares for all dumb creatures, especially me with CP.'

'CP?'

'Cerebral palsy. That's why my legs don't work properly. Luckily my hands aren't too bad, so they thought the piano would help develop coordination – as well as keep me here out of everyone's way. I actually love it here despite the manky fishy pongs, but it's kitten heaven. I can show you some little cuties out in the shelter – yes, a genuine World War Two air raid shelter in the garden. Gorgeous puppies in there, too. So how come you ended up here at 21 Braxted Avenue of all places?'

She sat on the sofa and, as we both stroked sleepy cats on our laps, I told her about the beach, my photos and cards for sale in town.

'I've never heard of stone-balancing,' she said. 'Mind you, balancing is clearly not one of my things – and I couldn't get down to that beach if I tried. Mr Rattacheck once took me and Gran round there in his speedboat. He's a wealthy guy who supports Gran's work. She calls Mr Rattacheck 'Mr Write-a-cheque!' He's a governor at school, too – you must have seen him in the paper and stuff. He once got into trouble for calling this an old-fashioned dozy little seaside town stuck in the past that needs bringing into the twenty-first century. Hashtag big mistake!'

I had no idea what she was going on about, probably because I've been called old-fashioned and dozy myself (by Uncle Calvin). I took out my phone and showed her some of my pictures. 'This one's my favourite,' I said. 'I took it from a distance to show all my stone piles together. How awesome is that?'

'Wow – I'm impressed. Can I enlarge it to see a bit of detail? I might just see how you've nailed all the rocks together.'

She expanded the image and held it up to her eyes. 'What's that, then?'

She pointed to a blurry shape at the foot of the cliff behind one of my stone piles. I hadn't noticed it before and I certainly hadn't seen it when I was there. Lying on the pebbles below the rocks was a pale pink handbag and, as the image sharpened, its chain strap became clearly visible. But that wasn't all. Beside it was what appeared to be a hand sticking up out of the sand, like a claw … its bent fingers glistening with trickles of blood.

FOUR

It might just be a crab doing a handstand or a weird bit of spiky seaweed, I kept telling myself. But every time I looked at that enlarged photo on my phone, I was convinced an adult human hand was sticking up from the sand at the foot of the cliff, close to the rocks. It was just like the top half of a hand, as if it was reaching up out of the churned-up sand, with only the top part of the thumb visible. Fuzzy though it was, I could see the four fingers, with bloody-looking trickles from the tips.

Could there really have been a body buried just metres from my stone-balancing? That seemed ludicrous – surely it couldn't happen. Why didn't other people on the beach notice something? There again, I'd deliberately chosen a spot tucked out of the way where no one went, apart from when they came over to admire my handiwork. They'd all taken their photos pointing in the other direction, with the sunlit sea as the background. My distance shot with the cliffs behind was the only one I had showing the hand. So my big question was: what should I do about it?

Sophie said I should show the police and let them sort it out. Mum wasn't so sure. For a start, she had other things on her mind and didn't want to call the police round to discuss 'a random fuzzy photo on a phone when there are bigger things to worry about'. But she had other reasons for telling me to forget it. She was worried she'd get into trouble for letting me clamber down to the beach on my own, unsupervised all day. So she made it clear I shouldn't make a fuss. I told her that was a bit ironic – my mum not fussing! 'Hey – that ought to go on the news. World Exclusive: Alison Rackman goes for the "no-fuss option". Will it ever happen again in our lifetime?'

She didn't see the funny side.

I thought some more about the uneasy feelings I had about my trip to the beach. I decided not to tell Mum any more. If I said anything about the guy on the cliff path, or how I'd fallen, she'd stop me going back – and that's exactly what I was desperate to do. I needed to return to the scene of the crime and see for myself what was really there.

I couldn't help thinking of the other puzzles I'd discovered on the cliff path, apart from that chunky spitty man puffing his way up with a rolled-up windbreak and his reaction when he saw me. There was also the pale pink sandal I saw in the undergrowth, with its spots of blood.

Suddenly the third thing flashed in my mind. How stupid – I'd totally forgotten.

I ran to get my backpack, unzipped the pocket and took out the wallet I'd found on the cliff. It was made of purple leather and had the letters EB embossed on a silver fastener that was undone. The compartments inside for banknotes and cash cards were empty, so was a plastic window for a name and address. I carefully looked through every section and discovered a slot behind a little pocket. Stuffed inside was a scrap of paper, which I carefully pulled out. It had been folded as if secretly inserted inside. Written in very neat handwriting was a poem, which I read a few times, but it didn't mean much – with what I assumed to be the poet's name at the end and a sort of extra comment added on:

Beginning and End

Morning starts the day,
Kissing like a tsunami.
Let the darkness fall…
Evening stars appear
In the blackest skies,
Ending all our fear…
Our dreaming never dies.

Ella Brookes

(If you find this
Don't think it must be
A fond farewell end)

Beware the oat crackers!

The paper was clean and dry, and the wallet was in good condition, so it probably hadn't been lying in the heather for long. I decided I'd give it to Mum to hand in when she went back to work. With nothing valuable inside it, I guessed a discarded wallet wasn't too important. More urgent, as far as I was concerned, was for me to go back to the beach first thing next morning. It was about time I checked things out close-up.

I woke early and left Mum a note to tell her I was off to the beach and that she needn't worry as I wasn't going in swimming and I'd take care. I wished her the best of luck at the hospital, where she was going for another blood test and a transfusion. I put the note on her bedside table, grabbed my backpack and ran out to get my bike.

It was one of those dazzling summer mornings and, although only just eight o'clock, the sun was already blazing down from a clear blue sky. I had no idea what to expect on the beach as I sped past Clifftop Caravan Park with all blinds still drawn, steered down to the cliff edge, left my bike under the same gorse bush as before and made my way down the cliff path. Once more I scrambled down between brambles and bracken, my trainers slipping and sliding in the dust. This time I slowed down at each twist and turn to stop myself nose-diving out of control. I paused about halfway down at the spot where I'd fallen before and seen the thuggy man jogging, sweating and spitting. I could see where I'd sprawled into nettles and where I'd found the wallet – but this time there was no pink sandal anywhere to be seen.

As it was now two days since I'd been down here, I was keen to see if my stones were still balancing. Although the sea and wind had been dead calm, a few high tides might have reached this far, so maybe my efforts had been washed away. As soon as I jumped onto the shingle, I ran along the narrow deserted beach with waves breaking close to the cliff.

It was great to see three of my stone towers still standing, with three mini-versions nearby that someone had tried to copy. But these weren't my reason for being here – so I walked past, on to the foot of the cliff. The stretch of sand where I had seen the hand in the photo was no longer churned-up but flat and smooth. That seemed odd, because the high tide only reached this far during storms or a full moon – and there had been neither. It looked as if the area had been deliberately smoothed over with a spade. Perhaps this spot had been used for playing cricket, as there were stump-holes poked into the sand, although strangely no sign of footprints. Taking a photo that I could compare with my last one, I was now convinced someone had been here to clean up the evidence – or maybe to bury it deeper. That's why I took a small plastic spade from my backpack. I had come prepared.

The sand was soft and dry, so I could dig easily. I soon scooped out a hole and began piling the loose sand to one side. Part of me dreaded what I might find, but the other part was desperate to uncover that hand, to prove to myself I hadn't been wrong. The scared part of me feared that any minute the hand would reach up, grab my throat and pull me down into the hole. Then the next stone balancer would come along and discover my big toe poking up from this bottomless grave of quicksand that swallows anyone who disturbs its buried victims – centuries of lost souls sucked down to their doom. Yikes. I took a deep breath and carried on digging.

Suddenly I gasped when I felt the spade hit something hard about thirty centimetres down. By frantically scraping away sand and grit, I nervously watched as a smooth surface appeared underneath. Instead of the cold skin of a corpse, I touched soft leather – a pale pink shoulder bag on a gold chain. I was sure it was the same bag that had been lying on the sand in my photo. I lifted it out and brushed all the sand off it, to find it was completely empty but in good condition. This hadn't been battered by the waves and washed up here – nor the pink right sandal buried beneath it, with a cork wedge heel, buckle fastening and elasticated strap. I had no doubt it matched the one I'd seen by the cliff path two days before as it, too, had specs of what looked like dried blood on the heel.

Both the bag and the sandal went straight in my backpack and I returned to digging, convinced I was about to unearth something more sinister. Soon I'd piled up a huge mound of loose sand above a deep, wide hollow. Bigger than a normal grave, the hole revealed no sign of grabbing zombie-fingers or the gruesome remains I thought I might find – not a hand anywhere to be seen.

I sat and stared with a mixture of relief and disappointment, as I was still none the wiser about the mysterious image in my photo.

Convinced nothing else was buried here, I began shovelling the mound back into the hole. It was then something silver caught my eye and I picked out from the fine sand a chain bracelet with a pearl heart attached to it. Carefully brushing it clean, I could just make out the letters EB engraved on the heart. I put it inside the shoulder bag and returned to filling-in the hole, only to see a pair of flip-flops suddenly appear beside it. I looked up, startled, to discover a woman in a big yellow sunhat smiling down at me.

'You've been so busy digging for treasure that you had no idea my dog was saying hello.' A Jack Russell was running around and yapping at my backpack. 'It's nice to see a young man able to blot out the world and concentrate so hard – just like with your stone towers over there. I watched you build them the other day and thought you're very clever. It's nice to see you've got rid of the stripy screen. Now I can see what you're up to. Let me know if you find gold!'

She chuckled, threw a ball for her dog to scamper after, waved and headed off along the beach. I didn't dare tell her I'd actually been looking for a dead hand!

My phone vibrated in my pocket and I saw two messages. One was from Mum telling me to be home by midday and the other was from Sophie.

Hi Fin. Gran says can you come round

today? She's made another yum cake and stopped boiling fish AT LAST! She's got loads of orders for your FAB cards and will pay YOU! Do you fancy taking a kitten to the vet? Love Soph x

I texted back immediately.

Hi Sophie – can I come str8 away? Need your advice. Just made big discovery. Fin

FIVE

As Mrs Boughtwood opened the front door, several cats darted out into the front garden. 'Thank goodness it's you, Finley,' she said. 'I thought it might be someone abandoning yet another kitten on the doorstep. It's been all go today. There's no need to come to the front door in future, dear. Just pop through the side gate and come straight in. You're one of the family now.'

She led me into a back room where Sophie was playing the piano in what they called the drawing room. 'I can't think why it's called that,' Sophie laughed, 'we've never done any drawing in here.'

Her gran soon put her right. 'It's called that because it's where people withdraw for relaxation – not that I ever have chance for that these days. I've got cats to clean out in the cattery. You're welcome to assist, Finley. Dirt trays to empty, fresh newspapers to put down and fish dinners to dish out. Just be careful of the tabby in the end cage as he's a bit wild.'

I actually enjoyed helping her. In fact, she left me the last five cats to sort out by myself. Apart from the manic tabby, I picked up each one for a cuddle and a chat. I don't think any of them answered back, but I told them why I was a bit worried about what I'd just found on the beach and it helped to sort out my thoughts.

Back in the drawing room, I told Sophie what I was thinking. I was sure there must be a connection between the hand in the photo, the wallet, the sandal and shoulder bag, the bracelet and the man on the cliff.

'To put it bluntly, I reckon there was a body buried there two days ago and now it's gone,' I said.

Sophie looked puzzled. 'Maybe the police found it and took it away. Or maybe it wasn't dead and managed to get up by itself. Then again, maybe I'm talking rubbish. But whatever happened, surely someone on the beach would have seen something and reported it?'

'That's what I thought,' I went on, 'but a woman down there just now made me wonder. When she told me it was nice to see I'd got rid of the stripy screen and she could now see what I was up to, I reckon she meant there had been a windbreak around the grave while a body was being buried or dug up. There were holes in the sand which I thought were from cricket stumps, but now I'm sure someone had put a screen up. It must have been that spitty guy I met on the cliff path. He had a stripy windbreak thing rolled round a shovel, so I reckon there's something dead weird going on with him. What you might call *fishy*.'

'Just like here.' Sophie pinched her nose. 'It smells like Gran's boiling up more scraps for the cats. A guy from the fishing boats brings her loads. In fact ... ' she paused and became more serious, 'if you're going to do some detective work, he might be worth talking to. He knows this coast, the tides and everything along the shore. Geoff goes out on the lifeboat, so always knows if any bodies get washed up or if anyone goes missing. But you'll probably find there's nothing to worry about. After all, I've checked online that no one's been reported missing or no suicide notes were found on the cliff top ... '

I remembered the purple wallet and took it from my backpack. 'What do you make of this?' I asked. Then I showed her the bracelet. Both had EB inscribed on them. Then I showed her the poem inside the wallet, with the name Ella Brookes.

'Wow, now this is getting interesting,' she said, her eyes lighting up. 'The plot thickens and I reckon this might be significant. I'm really into puzzles, so I'd like to help you get to the bottom of your little mystery, if you like.'

'Yeah – I would like.'

Although we'd met only two days ago, we were already getting on really well and I liked the idea of our doing some detective work together. Before we had chance to discuss our first line of enquiry, Sophie announced, 'I'll do some thinking, but first Gran's got a poorly kitten that needs to go to the vet. If I hold it in my lap, can you push me in my chair? It's only a couple of streets away and it would be great if you came with me.'

I sent my mum a text to tell her I'd be a bit late and happily agreed to push Sophie's wheelchair while she nursed a black fluffy kitten. The poor thing hardly moved, apart from hanging out its little pink tongue now and again.

Halfway down the street Sophie turned and looked up at me. 'Hey, how about when we're in the waiting room, we use sign language so we can talk about people without them knowing? Could be fun! Mrs Holmes taught me signing as I want to be a special needs nursery nurse.'

'You'd better show me,' I said. 'See if you make sense.'

Holding the kitten with her left hand, she held up her right. 'You really need to be facing me, but try this.' She showed three fingers, then just her little finger, then a clenched hand with two fingers slightly raised. 'What does that spell?' she asked.

'Could it be a three letter word beginning with F and ending in N?' I grinned.

'Got it! Not FUN, but your name.' She raised her hand to her mouth. 'That's good. It might be easier if we sit opposite each other at the vet's.'

When we got to the surgery, the kitten was sound asleep in Sophie's lap. The receptionist greeted her like an old friend and came out from behind the counter to kneel and stroke the kitten's head with a 'Bless his little heart'.

Another woman in uniform was mopping the floor

with strong disinfectant where a puppy with a bucket round its head had just drenched its owner's green suede shoes in a fit of panic.

No sooner had Sophie and I sat down in the waiting room and begun our signing experiment, when all heads turned towards the door marked Veterinary Surgeon. All of a sudden the door flew open and a man dragging a shaved bull terrier covered in stitches stormed out. Everyone cowered as the vet shouted after him. All pets in the room were quivering under seats and the vet made some kind of apology about the 'sudden outburst', as everyone in the waiting room tried to calm down from all the kerfuffle. Everyone apart from me. I sat frozen, trying to sign to Sophie just three words: 'That was him'.

She didn't realise what I meant – that the man charging past was the one I had met on the cliff; the same cropped head, tattooed left arm and boots with odd laces – one brown, one black. It was definitely him.

When it was our turn to go into the vet's surgery, I was still startled by the way the man had dragged his dog so aggressively. This time I'd seen his eyes – hostile and raging. The vet was totally the opposite – a kind and gentle man in a white coat and latex gloves who greeted us like old friends.

'And what can I do for you two young people? As if I need to ask. Another of Muriel Boughtwood's patients, it seems. And not a happy little fellow, either. Good to see you again, Sophie – and nice to meet you, young man. I'm Mr Massey.'

He shook me by the hand, then carefully examined the kitten, which hardly moved. 'Well, this little chap clearly has a nasty infection which I'll need to treat with antibiotics pretty swiftly. I'd also like to check him out more thoroughly and monitor him over the next twenty-four hours. He's got a temperature and I'm afraid he's going to need round the clock nursing, so we'd best keep him here and see how he is tomorrow. We'll do all we can, I promise.'

We were about to go when I plucked up courage to ask a question. 'Excuse me, Mr Massey but do you mind if I ask who that angry man was just now who stomped out dragging his dog?'

'I'm sorry about all that. It upset us all, I'm afraid. My assistant is reporting the matter in my office next door, so we hope that will be the last we see of him.'

Sophie was standing close to the door and I knew she was straining to hear what was being said inside.

'I'd love to work with animals,' I said.

'The animals are often delightful – it's their owners who give us nightmares!'

He shook my hand again as we left and I was so impressed by him that the first thing I said to Sophie outside was, 'I'd *so* like his job'.

'His name was Griffiths,' she said. 'Bryn Griffiths.'

I was confused. 'I thought he said he was Mr Massey.'

'No, the guy with the dog. I was listening at the door. Apparently that's the third time they've had to treat that animal and they think its injuries are from fights with badgers. Badger-baiting is illegal and Griffiths turned nasty when the vet threatened to report him.'

I felt sickened that somebody could be so cruel. 'I dread to think where that barbaric stuff happens.'

'The caravan park on the cliff. Griffiths runs it for Mr Rattacheck – the business guy I told you about who knows Gran. He'd be horrified if he knew that sort of thing happened at his caravan park.'

I was now convinced more than ever that this Griffiths man must be connected to what I'd discovered on the beach and I was determined to find out more.

Mrs Boughtwood's lemon drizzle cake was out of this world. We sat in the front room telling her how worried we were about the kitten. She seemed more worried about paying for his treatment.

'I might have to ask you two to go to the garden centre and empty the collecting boxes there. How about tomorrow?' She looked out of the window. 'And here's Geoff with the fish. He'll want paying as well. You'll just have to sell some more of your cards, Finley.' She went to answer the front door.

'Pass me my sticks,' said Sophie. 'I'm going to have a word with Geoff. Come and meet him.'

The man at the door wore navy blue overalls, a baseball cap and had a bushy ginger beard. A bucketful of fish scraps was at his feet while he counted the money he'd just been paid. 'All right Sophie, m'dear? Still playin' that pianer?'

'Geoff, do you happen to know a man called Bryn

Griffiths by any chance?' she asked. Her gran grabbed the bucket and disappeared indoors.

Geoff raised his bushy ginger eyebrows. 'Griffiths? Too right I do. He once came mackerel fishing with me. Never again. Why d'yer ask?'

'We just saw him at the vet's. He was really nasty in the waiting room.'

'He's often nasty,' Geoff nodded, 'even more so since his woman disappeared.'

'Disappeared?' I piped up.

'Gone. Missing,' he went on. 'I'm not surprised if she left him. They say he beat her.'

'He beat his wife?' Sophie said, horrified.

'She's not his missus. Partner. I've known the fiery Liz Baker for years. Mind you, she must be a saint to put up with him, I reckon.'

I wanted to know more, so I asked, 'When did she go missing?'

'Oh, not long. Only a couple of days ago. She'll be back. She's done it before. It's what you might call a stormy relationship. I know quite a lot about storms, believe me. They can soon die down, only to brew up again fiercer than before. And Bryn Griffiths gets very stormy indeed without Liz there to keep him calm.'

Back in the sitting room on our own, Sophie looked at me and smiled. 'I know what you're thinking, Fin. You think Bryn Griffiths bumped off his partner and dumped her on the beach.'

'So why would he dig her up again – and what happened to the body?'

Then I thought of the bracelet and wallet with the letters EB, which didn't fit in with the Liz Baker theory. Sophie must have read my mind.

'As Liz is short for Elizabeth, the wallet you found could have been hers.'

'Of course,' I gasped. 'Now it's all beginning to make sense!'

Sophie looked at her watch. 'Grandfather says it's three o'clock.'

I stared at her, confused.

'In the hall,' she giggled. 'Gran's grandfather clock just chimed three.'

'Yikes,' I said, leaping to my feet. 'My mum will go ballistic if I don't get back soon.'

'Come back as soon as you can,' Sophie smiled at me. 'I'm about to do some research and might have stuff to share anytime soon.'

Mum was lying on the sofa when I got home. The TV was on but she was dozing. She opened her eyes as I walked in the room.

'Where have you been? I've been worried. Why didn't you text?'

I told her I'd been with a friend. I knew that would make her sit up.

'A friend? Who is he?'

'*She*, actually. Sophie Boughtwood. We've just been to

the vet's with a kitten. I think I'd like to be a vet. Mr Massey was great.' I told her some of what I'd been up to, but nothing about the BHM as Sophie called it: Beach Hand Mystery. 'How are you, Mum?'

'Not too bad. I wish you'd text me more. You know I worry. Have you eaten?'

I told her I had and went on about all the animals at Mrs Boughtwood's.

'Is her husband Mr Boughtwood, the solicitor?' she asked.

'Yes. I've only seen him once as he's usually at work, although Sophie says he's over seventy. He always wears a spotty bow tie and his wife calls him MOTH, which is short for Man of the House. He's got an awesome billiard table in the drawing room where Sophie plays the piano.'

I knew that would impress her. 'I'm really pleased you're mixing more, love.'

I asked her how her blood transfusion went. 'Quite well,' she said. 'I felt a bit better afterwards, but my blood count was really low. They're trying to find me a donor.'

'Is that because you need more blood?' I asked.

'Bone marrow,' she sighed. 'I need a transplant apparently. Otherwise ... ' she looked away, but I knew she was struggling not to get upset. I sat beside her on the sofa and held her hand.

'Don't worry, Mum. They'll find someone. I'll look after you.' I squeezed her fingers and smiled, even though a tear was rolling down my cheek when I said, 'If all else fails, I know a really nice vet.'

She laughed.

Sophie told me to sit down and pay close attention because she had information from her latest investigation on the BHM case. I muttered something about her being as bossy as her gran, but she ignored me and carried on excitedly. 'I couldn't find anything significant for Liz Baker, but I think this looks interesting. I thought I'd look at who the poet Ella Brookes might be – and it looks like she might be this Ella Brookes who's twenty six and a freelance writer, but also a waitress at the seaside in the holiday season. She studied journalism at university and is on the lookout for a good scoop, whatever that means.'

Sophie showed me Ella's latest Facebook page on a laptop:

Time to BREAK THE SILENCE

Watch this space for when I spill the beans, blow the whistle, stick my neck out, mix my metaphors, tell it as it is and risk breaking the silence. More soon.

> *'Silence becomes cowardice when occasion demands speaking out the whole truth and acting accordingly.'*
>
> (Mahatma Gandhi)

Like Comment Share

My heart sank. What had this got to do with anything?

'I don't see how this connects with the poem I found in the wallet or anything else for that matter,' I said, a bit too grumpily, so I tried to sound jollier with 'I think you've followed a false lead, chief inspector.' I was disappointed that she was getting us nowhere.

Sophie didn't give up. 'I thought you might say that, sergeant – but take a look at Ella's picture.' She sat back looking very smug.

Smiling up at me from the screen was a pretty young woman with short jet-black hair, dark brown eyes and wearing a purple top. It was one of those posed mug-shots with her chin in her right hand, and the elbow resting casually on a table. It was the sort of picture a writer or artist might pose for.

'She looks very nice,' I sighed, 'but you'll have to do better that this, inspector. Notice you've now been demoted from chief inspector as a result of your unsatisfactory research.'

Sophie remained as cool as a cucumber, enlarged the picture and said with a smug grin, 'In that case, constable – you need to take a closer look.'

My jaw dropped when I saw what was shining very clearly on Ella's wrist. It was the exact bracelet I had found buried in the sand.

SIX

'I don't suppose the police will be interested, but I can give them a call if you like,' Mrs Boughtwood said while scrubbing out a cat basket. 'They all know me at the station as "the animal woman" as I'm always dealing with lost or found pets for them. I expect they call me far worse when I complain that they never do enough to catch the cruel people who harm or abandon their pets.'

Sophie had told her gran I'd found a shoulder bag, wallet and bracelet on the beach and suggested reporting it in case someone tried to claim them. The picture of Ella Brookes wearing the same bracelet might have been of interest to the police, we thought. We were wrong.

Mrs Boughtwood was on the phone for ages, probably chatting about all kinds of random stuff. In the end, she said the police had made a note of the bracelet but they already had a long list of lost and found things reported on the beach during the height of the season. They told her the biggest culprit was the sea itself, which is in the habit of snatching and hiding stuff twice a day when the tide comes in (and out) along the shore.

The police didn't even want to see the 'hand in the sand' photo. Apparently they get sent hundreds of pictures of fake body parts sticking out of mud, sand, cesspits and graveyards every year. Ninety-nine percent are hoaxes and they just don't have the manpower to investigate jokers who inflate rubber gloves and stick them in the ground, or upturned boots on legs poking up from bogs, or manikins' hands stuck in sand to look like they're groping their way out of a beach grave. Basically, the police didn't want to know about my buried body theory. We were on our own.

'Fair enough,' Sophie said. 'We'll get to the bottom of this all by ourselves.'

'That's fine by me,' I cheered, as we high-fived, but I feared we'd get nowhere and it might be best to forget all about Operation BHM, as we still called it. I was now beginning to doubt my own instincts. The only thing making me want to continue was that we might just manage to help stop the thuggy Bryn Griffiths do any more harm to dogs or people. I couldn't get his mean face and cruel eyes out of my head.

Sophie was still busy on her phone. 'I've now found Ella's email address, so I'm sending her a message so she can get in touch if she's lost a bracelet or wallet.'

I didn't say anything, but I was more convinced they

belonged to Liz Baker and that the dreaded Griffiths had done something terrible to her. Before we decided what our next move would be, I got a text from Mum.

> Sorry Fin – just had a phone call and need to tell you some news asap. Please come home.

When I got to our road, my stomach churned at the sight of a red Skoda parked at a weird angle, with one wheel up on the path outside our gate. The dented front bumper still hadn't been repaired since New Year's Day, so I knew instantly it was Uncle Calvin's.

I'm useless at sensing an atmosphere in a room but even I could tell Mum had been crying and Uncle Calvin was having a big sulk. Their body language screamed 'tension' as they both sat stiffly without talking, faces like thunder and Mum's plate of strawberries left untouched, swimming in melted ice cream. Uncle Calvin sat huffily in scruffy old jeans and a gross Hawaiian shirt with a grubby vest bulging through a missing button at his massive stomach. Most of the hair on his head had disappeared, apart from a few days' stubble, like a rash over his double chin. I couldn't help thinking his puffy cheeks looked like tufty coconut shells.

'Hi, Uncle Calvin,' I said, as cheerfully as I could. 'How's life with you?'

'Don't ask,' he grunted miserably. 'This isn't a social visit. It's business. Serious business. It affects you, Fin – so you need to pay very careful attention. Understand?'

He glared right into my eyes and I was relieved when Mum butted in. 'Let me handle this, Calvin. You can have your say afterwards.'

I sat on the arm of a chair by the door where I could see them both and watch their faces carefully. 'Go on then, I'm all ears.' I grinned and folded my arms, trying to look relaxed, while inside I was knotting-up because I knew this might get stressy. Already my jokey manner was annoying Uncle Calvin as he bristled and looked away, muttering to himself grumpily.

'Fin, let me explain.' Mum looked directly at me as calmly as she could, although her wet eyes were red, her face was blotchy and her neck was mottled with yellowy-green bruises.

'My blood cells aren't working properly, so if they don't do something soon I'll get sick. It means they've got to zap all my bad blood cells with chemicals to get rid of the lot, then start my system all over again by giving me new stem cells that will get my blood and body cells working properly. That's the theory. They want to give me the first dose of chemo next week while they try and find a donor to match my own stem cells. That's the tricky bit, apparently.'

'It's no good beating about the bush, Ali,' Uncle Calvin broke in, leaning forward in his chair and clasping his hands firmly as if to underline the next bit. 'There's a big fat elephant in the room and it won't go away.'

I so wanted to add, 'Yes, Uncle Calvin and it's you, seeing as you've put on so much weight and I wish you'd go home.' Instead I sat silently, just watching. After a pause he continued. 'The truth of the matter, Fin, is that I see this as blackmail and I've told your mum it's as if she's holding me to ransom with a dirty great gun to my head. She's called me here to tell me she won't last six months unless I go with her to the haematologist bloke at some city hospital and get ripped open for my bone marrow, in case there's an outside chance I can save her.'

Mum interrupted, looking even more upset. 'It's nothing like that, Calvin. It's only a blood test at this stage. They say it's non-invasive and low-risk. There's a one-in-four chance a brother or sister is a full match and I just thought you would … '

'Well you thought wrong. The bottom line is, I don't do hospitals and never have. Needles and blood stress me out. I can't do it, Ali. I'm sorry and that's all there is to it. Find someone else to be cannibalised for their body parts.'

I looked at Mum for her reaction, as I couldn't believe what he was saying. She just stared, unable to speak.

'What if was the other way round?' I asked him. 'Would you want Mum to be your donor if you were ill, Uncle Calvin?'

'Of course not. I wouldn't expect it and I wouldn't ask. And if I did, I'd make sure I paid her. After all, even if I did agree to be abused by blood-sucking vampires in white coats, what's in it for me?'

That's when I lost it. I stood up, swore, shouted all kinds of stuff about him being too selfish to rescue his own sister and I stormed out. I couldn't bear to face the other elephant in the room right then. But I knew it was there, flapping its ears and trunk in my face: *If Mum was going into hospital, what would happen to me?* I already had very firm views about that subject. I'd rather be taken into care than have to go and live with Uncle Calvin.

'You don't have to worry about that, Fin,' Mum said later, after Uncle Calvin had gone off in a huff to the pub and we'd both calmed down a bit.

'He's kindly agreed to come and baby-sit if necessary. He and Jasmine are prepared to move in for however long it takes. Everything will be fine.'

That's when I erupted again, stomped out of the house and cycled back to see Sophie.

'What's the matter?' Sophie asked. 'You seem really quiet this evening. Have you lost your sparkle?'

I didn't tell her I might have inherited Intermittent Explosive Disorder, as I seemed to be losing my cool more and more, fearing I was turning into Uncle Calvin. I told her everything else, how I was seething inside and really worried about Mum going into hospital.

'Hospitals aren't that bad,' she said. 'I've spent most of my life going in and out of the places. I've had more operations on my legs than I can remember. They'll get her sorted, don't you worry.'

At least she seemed to understand when I told her about Uncle Calvin, and I even felt a bit better after telling her how upset and angry I was. Playing with a litter of puppies helped, too – then cleaning out all the cat pens in the garage. Even the wild tabby seemed to listen to me moaning away.

Sophie was smiling from ear to ear when I returned to the sitting room. 'Good news and bad news,' she announced. 'Bad first. No reply yet from my email to Ella Brookes. Good news is that she's definitely the owner of the wallet. Look, I found her on Twitter. She's posted a picture of the poem.'

She showed me Ella's last entry just a few days ago.

Ella Brookes
On a mission. Can't say more in case they see this.
If the worst happens, see below.

Beginning and End

Morning starts the day,
Kissing like a tsunami.
Let the darkness fall ...
Evening stars appear
In the blackest skies,
Ending all our fear ...
Our dreaming never dies.

Beware the carrot cakes!

'Does that really help?' I asked. 'What does it tell us?'

'It tells us who her followers are. One of them looks like a close friend called Lian Sung, so I've just sent her a message to see if we can find out anything. Impressed?'

'I guess so. I hope it helps!'

She told me to look on the bright side and to believe that things can always get better. Somehow, I knew that was unlikely when it came to Uncle Calvin.

I couldn't forget he was still the 'lurking predator' Grandad always warned me about – and I knew the most cunning predator strikes when you least expect.

SEVEN

Mum lay on her bed beside scorching red curtains pulled across her closed window, hiding the dazzling midday sun gleaming over the sea. Her room was hot, very still and bathed in shimmering pink light.

'I've brought you some strawberries,' I said quietly. 'Uncle Calvin's gone out again. It's just us here now.'

She stirred, her face pale and strained, with dark rims under her hollow eyes. A box of tissues beside her was full of blood-soaked scrunches.

'Thanks love. Just put them on the side there. I'm not supposed to eat them really. My immune system is in meltdown, so no germs or maggots allowed.' She tried to smile, but the effort seemed too much.

'Have you eaten something, Fin? Sorry I'm neglecting you today. I seem to have slept the morning away. I should be out there enjoying the sun. I hope you're not getting bored all by yourself.'

I told her I'd been busy printing off a lot more cards with different designs and messages inside. I'd written a sort of poem in a fancy font, then set out a spreadsheet to record sales, expenses and profits of my new business enterprise for charity. I guessed she thought that seemed nerdy, as her eyes remained closed and she spoke very slowly, as if she was slipping back to sleep. 'You never cease to amaze me, Fin.'

'I'm sorry,' I said.

She lifted her head slightly but struggled to speak. 'Don't be,' she sighed at last, closing her eyes again with heavy breaths. I sat beside her on the bed and silently watched her eyelids for a few minutes before whispering into her ear, 'I mean it. I'm sorry, Mum. I'm really sorry.'

There was no reaction as I looked down at her lifeless hands and blurted, 'Sorry for all that stuff I said earlier.'

I wasn't sure if she was still listening but I went on, although I really struggled.

'I'm sorry for everything. You've got enough to worry about without me being a pain. It's just that … '

She reached out and touched my hand, her eyes spilling tears. 'You don't deserve all this.'

I took a deep breath and clasped her fingers. 'No one does, Mum. I'm sorry I've been a bit selfish sometimes. It's just that … ' Now tears filled my eyes, too. 'It's just that I'm fed up of getting knocked down all the time, just when I think things are going to be okay.'

I thought of my stone-balancing and wished I could get everything at home sorted and balanced like my efforts on the beach. I'd done all I could to keep rebuilding every time things went wrong, but now it was all crashing around me. I tried to explain. 'With balancing stones I feel in control and can stay really calm. But here it's different. Sometimes it's like there's screaming getting louder in my head. Right now it feels like even the stones are screaming, too.'

'I understand,' she said slowly, her eyes still closed. 'It's not fair, is it, love?'

I rested my head beside hers on the damp pillow and said very softly, 'I don't know what to do, Mum. I'm scared. I want everything to be like it used to be. I want to make things just right. That's not too much to ask, is it?'

She didn't answer this time. She remained very still, her breathing becoming slower. Gently getting up off the bed, I backed away, watching her sleeping till I reached the door. I turned to go out, then glanced back one more time. She looked peaceful, but so helpless that I wanted to scream louder than ever. I knew the strawberries beside her would remain untouched and, for the first time, I realised our time together, just like the summer, was slowly slipping away. All I could do was run to my bedroom, throw myself on my bed and sob as silently as I could manage.

'I'm afraid we're a bit strapped for cash,' Mrs Boughtwood smiled as soon as I walked in the kitchen, as though she was telling me the best news in the world. 'The vet bills, food bills and other expenses have all come together and leave us short this month, so I have a proposal to make, Finley. Seeing as you're so good at helping our petty cash with your lovely cards, how about if we sell some at our front gate, as well as postcards for tourists and all sorts of bits and pieces I've found in the spare bedroom? I've had a massive clear-out. You'll have the lion's share of the profits from your cards, of course.'

'You mean like a car boot sale?' I asked.

'No dear,' she smiled again, which confused me even more, because the mood on her face never seemed to match what she was saying. 'It can't be a car boot sale, can it? We haven't got a car for a start. It will be a gate sale of your photos and my bric-a-brac.'

I had no idea what that was, but I daren't ask as she could be scary when she went off on one of her lectures. It was a relief when Sophie interrupted with, 'Why don't you ask for a loan from Mr Write-a-check, Gran?'

'It's funny you should say that, Sophie. I've asked him round for drinks and nibbles later and I'll try all my charm on him. It would be nice if Finley could be here, too. His angelic eyes could charm the birds from the trees.'

Sophie giggled, her gran gave an even sicklier smile and I must have looked more confused than ever.

'I'll also invite Trevor from next door who's a photographer for The Gazette. Mr Rattacheck won't be able to resist a photo opportunity, seeing as he's standing for mayor and needs to make a good impression. If he's seen as a supporter of helpless animals he'll be quids-in, and so shall we. You see, Finley, you have to be crafty to get what you want in this life.'

Sophie nodded enthusiastically. 'And I've got another great idea,' she said. 'Fin could show his stone pictures in the newspaper – free advertising! If he's shown holding a cute puppy as well, we'll get queues at the gate to buy his cards. How about it, Fin?'

I liked the idea of mass-producing even more of my cards to make some cash, so I happily agreed. Mrs Boughtwood seemed very pleased with herself. 'That's marvellous. And so was the call from the vet just now. That little kitten you took in for me is much better and can come home, if you'd like to collect it. We could even ask Trevor to put the story in the paper with a headline like *Stone-Balancer Helps Save Kitten's Life!* As the money you'll raise with a shop at the gate will help pay the vet, you could become a local hero, Finley.'

I smiled and gave a low bow. 'Anything you say, Mrs Boughtwood.'

In fact, I was pleased to have something to do to take my mind off things at home – something to calm the swirling and screaming in my head. At the same time, she had just planted a thought in my brain. Perhaps there was a possible answer to the big question hanging over me like a darkening cloud. I'd keep it in mind if the worst happened.

I'd never seen such an old bike, let alone ridden one.

Mrs Boughtwood said she'd had it over fifty years and the large basket on the front had carried many kittens to and from the vet's in that time. As Sophie had an appointment at the clinic, I offered to collect the kitten on my own – by wobbling down the road on the old bike. Inside the basket, Mrs Boughtwood had wrapped a hot water bottle in a woolly jumper to give the patient a snug ride home. The bike was weird to steer as the basket didn't turn with the handlebars. The frame was heavy and clunky and I knew I didn't look cool riding an old woman's ancient bike. At the first junction I came to I turned left, but it felt like the basket was going straight ahead so I slammed on the brakes and skidded into the kerb. I fell onto the path and grazed my knee, just as a topless bus full of sightseers passed by. I felt really embarrassed, dreading I'd end up on YouTube and go viral.

As soon as I picked up the kitten, it tried to climb up my shirt onto my shoulder to nuzzle my neck. Mr Massey showed me how to give tablets by gently squeezing open the kitten's jaws, placing a tiny pill on the back of its pink tongue, closing its mouth and stroking its throat. Hey presto, tablet gone! He told me I was a natural vet and should make sure I did that three times a day, then the kitten would be as right as rain. I felt so chuffed with myself.

'We're very lucky that little chap has pulled through,' Mr Massey said. 'There must be something magic about him. Maybe you should call him Merlin.'

I put Merlin (as I called him from then on) into the

basket where he snuggled into the jumper. I pushed the bike down the street as I didn't want to risk falling off again. My new passenger was far too important for that. In fact, I had already grown attached to little Merlin, so I'd decided to ask if I could keep him.

When I got back to Mrs Boughtwood's house, I had to put Merlin in a basket in the spare bedroom, then help take bowls of olives and dips into the garden. Mr Boughtwood was working late at the office, so I was given one of his bow ties to wear as I was to be 'Man of the House' for the evening. That meant pouring drinks and smiling a lot. Sophie had her electric wheelchair so she could whizz around with a tray of crisps and celery sticks. Mrs Boughtwood fussed around in a long black skirt and silky blouse, then got very excited when a white Mercedes with the number plate ER1 parked outside the front gate.

'He's here. That's Mr Rattacheck's car,' she said, hurrying down the drive to greet him.

'Gran goes a bit over the top,' Sophie smiled. 'After one glass of fizz she gets all flirty. It's good entertainment value. You must put this in your blog.'

It had been Sophie's idea that I should keep a sort of diary each day. It was really a record of events on my phone – nothing posted online. Day One was when we first met – the day I made the discovery on the beach. Day Five was when I named Merlin, promised him I'd become a vet and, that evening, I first met Mr Rattacheck.

The great man wore a stripy pink designer shirt with the top buttons undone to show a leather choker with ivory tusk. The red sleeves of a slinky jumper were draped over his shoulders, while wine-coloured trousers, fluorescent pink socks and classy red leather shoes were all shouting 'Look at me'. To me, they screamed 'Naff' and I wondered why his wife let him out looking so flashy and uncool. Sophie just called him a super-rich chav. Even though it was evening, he had expensive-looking sunglasses perched on his head, probably to hide his thinning wispy brown hair.

'Muriel, my darling, you look gorgeous,' he said grandly, kissing the back of her hand and following on with a string of kisses up her arm.

'Oh, you're making me blush, Mr Rattacheck.' Mrs Boughtwood giggled like a little girl who'd won first prize at a gymkhana.

'Call me Eros,' he replied, leading her into the garden. 'I let my favourite ladies call me by my first name. You see, I'm half-Greek, half-Polish.

'And which half is which?' Mrs Boughtwood guffawed and he did the same. Sophie and I caught each other's eye and laughed, just as more people began to arrive.

'Despite his fashion sense, he's a great guy,' Sophie told me, as we fetched more glasses from the kitchen. 'He's larger than life with a mega personality. He's the only one I know who can make my gran quiver in her shoes.'

As soon as the man from next door arrived with his camera, Mrs Boughtwood called everyone together and made a speech.

'It gives me great pleasure to welcome friends and

neighbours to our animal centre. At twenty one Braxted, we are attempting to raise extra funds to support sick and neglected pets in our town, as well as the ongoing work to buy guide dogs for the blind. Young Finley here has come up with a wonderful scheme to raise cash by donating some of the proceeds from his card-making business – some of them are on sale here now. Soon there will be a shop at our gate that he and Sophie will run for us. Their help will save kittens like this one, just safely back from the vet's after being found abandoned and very sick – now named Merlin.'

I held him up and everyone clapped as he licked my hand. Before the clapping stopped, Mr Rattacheck took over. 'Ladies and gentlemen, as a local businessman and councillor, I am delighted to make another donation to this worthy cause and invite you all to support young Finley and Sophie in their mini-enterprise shop at the gate. As a 'thank you' to them, I will offer to take them on a trip along the coast in my speedboat anytime soon. So how about three cheers and a photo for the Gazette?'

There was more applause, a lot of posing and camera flashes – which Merlin was totally unbothered by. I felt so chuffed when Mr Rattacheck shook me by the hand and said, 'You're a fine young fellow with a big heart and I love those stone-balance pictures. I will buy some to sell in my restaurant and club. Make me two hundred as a starter. Don't forget to print a copyright sign on them. Bring them to The Actor's Creak tomorrow at two o'clock and we'll go for a spin.'

By the time everyone had gone home and the great Mr Rattacheck had glided off, blowing kisses from his Mercedes, we'd packed everything away under a bright pink sky and crimson sun. Sophie and I were still laughing at her gran, who was singing and waving her arms as she drained the last bottle of Prosecco.

'I have cleared the spare bedroom and it's spotless. Boxes of books, comics, china and all sorts are ready for pricing up. How about starting our sale on Monday, my dears? By then we'll be in the paper.'

We happily agreed and she cheered before dancing off into the kitchen to wash up. As soon as we were alone, Sophie grabbed her phone and waved it in front of me.

'Hey, you know I sent a message to Ella Brookes' friend called Lian? Well, I've just had a reply from her. She says they were at university together.'

I didn't like to say that I'd almost forgotten about Operation BHM and that maybe we should let it drop. Now I had other things to think about, I began to wonder if I'd been wrong about all that stuff on the beach. What Sophie said next made me think again.

'Lian wants to come and see us. She must think we're important as she's coming all the way from Glasgow – this weekend.'

When I got home there was no one about and thankfully no sign of Uncle Calvin. Mum's bedroom was empty, so I assumed she must have gone out somewhere. I was surprised she hadn't sent me a text or left a post-it note on my bedroom door. I sent her a text to tell her I was home and hoped she was feeling better. Then I set to work printing more cards. I once saw a poster outside a church showing huge rocks with the message: 'If they remain silent, the very stones will cry out. *Luke 19.40.*' I thought that was cool for one of my pictures, so I tweaked it and then wrote a short poem that I called 'Breaking the Silence', which sort of said how I was feeling a bit like the stones in my picture.

If I remain silent, the very stones will cry out.
Luke 19.40

Breaking the Silence

Even when the stones call out
Who will hear their cry?
Unbalanced, petrified we shout;
Unsilenced, screaming 'WHY?'
Fin Rackman © (The Stone Balancer)

What is joy without sorrow?
What is success without failure?
What is a win without a loss?
What is health without illness?
You have to experience each if you are to appreciate the other.
There is always going to be suffering;

> It's how you look at your suffering, how you deal with it, that will define you. (Mark Twain)
>
> *Fin Rackman © (The Stone Balancer)*

I was so busy folding each card and putting them into envelopes that I didn't notice Mum standing beside me.

'Hey, where did you come from all of a sudden, Mum?'

'I've just got your text, love. Sorry, I was in the spare bedroom. I've been tidying it and getting it ready. I must have fallen asleep half-way through.'

I said it must be the latest fashion to clear out spare bedrooms. She didn't say anything other than, 'Nice cards, Fin. That quote is a bit close for comfort.'

'So what's up, Mum?' I asked. 'Anything happening? How's everything?'

She sat down on my bed and looked straight at me. 'I'm being admitted to the Haematology Unit at City Hospital on Sunday afternoon, to begin treatment on Monday. It's all happening a bit quicker than I thought.'

I wasn't sure what to say. I so wanted to tell her about Mr Rattacheck, his big order for my cards, the promised trip in his speedboat and the shop Sophie and I would be running on Monday – but I knew Mum's hospital treatment was far more important. 'What will they do to you?' I asked.

'I have to have a heart scan first to make sure I'm fit enough, then I'll be fitted with something called a Hickman line that's connected near my collar bone – into the vein above my heart. It's to get the chemicals into my body that will destroy all my bad blood cells. It will get rid of my hair, too.'

I must have stared, imagining her without her lovely thick black hair, as she looked down to avoid my eyes. The thought of her being bald and so frail really got to me, but I managed to tell her not to worry as I'd stick by her all the way. Even though she'd be miles away, I said I could easily get a train to go over to visit her.

'I'm afraid not, love,' she said. 'No one is allowed near me as I'll be at risk from infection. I have to be locked away till they can get my white blood cells, called neutrophils, to increase. I'll have a condition called neutropenia, which means I'll be at risk of infections. Fingers crossed they'll find a donor for when I've finished the chemo, so I can get some stem cells to fire up my immune system again. I'm dreading it all, but at least they're on my case at last. Then I'll be back to my old jolly self – and nagging you to death.'

She tried to smile, but I could see the fear in her eyes. Even so, I had to ask the dreaded question. 'How long will you be in hospital, Mum?'

'I'm not sure. It could be two weeks or maybe more. But don't worry, love – you won't have to go away to stay with Uncle Calvin. I've made other arrangements.'

I suppose I should have looked pleased, but I feared what was coming next. 'The mountain will come to Mohammed.' She put her hand on mine.

She must have realised that I hadn't understood what she meant exactly, as she smiled and added, 'I know how you don't want to go and stay with Uncle Calvin, so the good news is, I've persuaded him, with the help of a bit of cash. For the next couple of weeks I'm paying him and Jasmine to stay in the spare bedroom and look after you. They're moving in tomorrow.'

EIGHT

Friday was another scorching August morning. I ate breakfast in the garden and watched the last of the seagull chicks fly from the nest on the roof next door. It returned from time to time to be fed by one of its parents coughing up something gross for it to swallow. It put me off my strawberries and Coco-pops, but not as much as the thought of Uncle Calvin and the dreadful Jasmine moving in. She could be even grumpier than him, and once they started drinking (sometimes a few beers at breakfast) they could be unbearable. When they came to stay at New Year she drank so much she passed out naked in the bathroom. Unfortunately it was me who found her, and it's like my head has been messed up ever since. Because she's so enormous we couldn't move her till she'd sobered up. Mum covered her in blankets and we just had to carry on as normal, trying to ignore the elephant in the bathroom.

I was dreading having to spend the next two weeks without Mum at home. I wasn't just worried about *her*, but also about the invasion of the baby-sitters from hell. I knew it would be *me* looking after *them*, rather than the other way round. Mum didn't realise how much I disliked them but, as I'd upset her if I said anything, I kept quiet.

Trying to take my mind off the following week, I set to work clearing out the shed. As Mrs Boughtwood had promised I could have Merlin when he'd fully recovered, I wanted to make sure he'd have his own snug den in our garden. He probably wouldn't be allowed indoors at first, till I could convince Mum to let me have him.

Before long I'd made a cosy bed on a shelf at the window, where he could doze or look out at the world. I also adjusted a plank in the corner as a sort of cat flap. It was more of a gaping hole with a flap of sack pinned over it by the time I'd finished hacking out a Merlin-sized gap. I couldn't wait to introduce him to his new deluxe home with his own personal entrance – a smart penthouse suite shared with my bike, stacks of flower pots and a rusty old lawn mower.

After I'd packaged up all the new cards for Mr Rattacheck, I made Mum a sandwich and we sat outside under the apple tree in the blazing midday sun. She laughed when I told her I'd used half a tub of antibacterial hand scrub to make sure my fingers and her food were super-safe from 'pesky micro-organisms with attitude'.

'I'm going to miss you so much next week, Fin. I'll

have my iPad, so make sure you Skype as often as you can, so I can see your face and hear your voice.'

I laughed. 'I've no idea what that must be like!'

'More precious than you can possibly imagine.'

She insisted on smothering me in sun lotion and lectured me about wearing a life-jacket when I went out on the speedboat. I moaned about her nagging but we laughed a lot between unspoken pauses, when I couldn't help thinking this could be the end of something special that might never return.

Desperate not to be late for our sea trip, I got to Mrs Boughtwood's with plenty of time to spare. Sophie was ready and waiting, just as excited as me.

'Phones at the ready,' she beamed. 'I want to record the look on your face when we reach full speed over the waves. It could be a bit choppy out there. We'll have to be strapped in – health and safety.'

I told her I was a professional stone-balancer with amazing powers at keeping steady and controlling my inner equilibrium. She laughed, 'Just remember that – when you go flying off the back of the boat. I'll probably fall off before the engine starts!. Unlike you, I can't balance much, but I'm a Libra and meant to be a well-balanced character. I may wobble physically, but mentally I reckon I'm as steady as your stones. Just remember when you're unsure about Operation BHM that my Libran instincts are never wrong. At the moment they tell me you're an unhappy bunny, Fin. What's up?'

I began to tell her my worries about Mum, then my dread of her brother and his partner. But I didn't tell her everything. I didn't tell her what I was secretly planning.

Her gran burst in, gabbling so fast and jumping from one random thing to the other – which made me make a huge gaff that we laughed about for ages.

'I'm glad you're here, Finley. Would you like to help us tomorrow by pricing up goods for the sale, as well as going with Sophie to the garden centre to fetch the money from their collection boxes? Your kitten is scampering around all over the place – so much so that in the night he woke me and I decided I'd write a book of my memoirs called 'A Kitten on the Doorstep'. I expect Sophie's told you we're all a bit sad today as Paddy's dead. He died in the night.'

I completely missed the thread of what she was saying, but the last part took me by surprise. 'Oh, that's terrible,' I said. 'If I'd known, I'd have brought you some flowers and a card.' They both looked at me with puzzled faces and Mrs Boughtwood gave me one of her scary grins. 'That's going a bit far, dear. He was a good age for a hamster and it wasn't unexpected.'

'You weren't paying attention, were you?' Sophie giggled. 'Gran said 'Paddy's dead.'

'Oh, that's a relief,' I answered. 'I thought she said your dad is dead!'

They roared with laughter and I felt really foolish, but Sophie came back with what I thought was a good joke. 'It could have been worse. My last hamster caused a major accident when he died.'

I gave a puzzled stare but she added with a smirk, 'He fell asleep at the wheel!'

The Actor's Creak was a smart white-washed (or more accurately cream-washed) building on the seafront, among the Victorian grand hotels. It had once been a theatre, but was now a restaurant and tapas bar as well as a conference centre, with expensive sea-view apartments above it. I had never set foot inside the place before and I was really impressed as I trod on the thick carpet through the revolving door. Mr Rattacheck was behind the reception desk talking to a man in a red waistcoat and bowtie. When he saw me he immediately came whizzing towards me like a missile.

'My friend, I have an hour to take you for a spin.' He shook my hand and looked at the bag in my hand. 'Are they my cards?' He flicked through them, 'Perfect. Perfect.' Turning to the man behind the desk, he clicked his fingers and called, 'Get me two hundred in twenties.'

He led me over to collect my payment. I'd never had so much money in my pocket before. When he saw the look of surprise on my face as he instructed the man at the desk to sell the cards for four pounds each, he smiled. 'Business is business, my friend.' He fetched a key ring from a hook behind the counter and marched ahead, pushing through the revolving doors into the dazzling sun, where Sophie sat waiting in the heat and wagging a finger.

'I don't think much of your fancy doors, Mr Rattacheck – they're not very wheelchair-friendly.'

He kissed her hand with, 'No worries – there's a side door with a ramp.'

She didn't give in. 'So I'm only fit for the tradesman's entrance am I? When I become mayor I'll make some new rules round here.'

'I guess you have a point,' he smiled, 'but I'll be mayor first.' He pushed her wheelchair along a side road towards the harbour. Half the people we passed waved or spoke to Mr Rattacheck, as though he was a celebrity on a stroll with a couple of awestruck kids.

'Tell me, Mr Rattacheck,' Sophie asked, 'why is your restaurant called The Actor's Creak?'

'Simple,' he grinned. 'Two reasons. It was a theatre long ago and it's haunted by a Victorian actor. Some nights we hear his footsteps and creaking floorboards coming from the old stage. The second reason is my touch of genius. If you care to rearrange the letters of Eros Rattacheck you get The Actor's Creak. Clever or what?'

Even though I'm not very good with anagrams and I couldn't work it out without paper, I couldn't help being impressed.

We were soon on a wooden jetty in the blazing sun. Boats of all kinds were moored around us, with a few holidaymakers out in rowing boats or fishing from dinghies. We looked down on a sleek white speedboat with cream leather seats; two in the front behind a curved smokey-grey windscreen and what looked like a luxury sofa in the back. A jagged red and yellow streak ran down the outside, with the name in silver: ACE SHOT TRACKER.

'Is this your speedboat?' I asked, my eyes bulging.

'You bet,' he said proudly. 'The clue's in the name.'

'Hey, I've just worked it out,' Sophie waved excitedly, 'It's an anagram of Eros Rattacheck. How ACE is that?'

'I'm totally gobsmacked,' I said, and he laughed as he jumped down onto the deck. He reached up to Sophie. 'I'll lift you down and Finley can pass down your wheelchair for stowing in the space behind the rear seat.'

As soon as she was onboard, Sophie was taking photos in all directions. She even zoomed in on Mr Rattacheck's cool black-and-white checked leather shoes.

'I call them my yachting shoes – Rattacheck's yachter-checks,' he grinned. When I sat beside Sophie in the back she tapped my arm and began signing. 'We'll have to sign to each other if we want to talk above the noise of this engine. She raised both hands above her head, her palms facing outwards, 'It's awesome!'

We put on our orange lifejackets as the mooring ropes were untied and we drifted clear of the jetty. Then, standing proudly at the wheel in his bright green silk shirt with matching designer lifejacket and sunglasses, Mr Rattacheck turned to give the thumbs-up, before starting the engine with the press of a button. I could smell the fumes as the boat vibrated and moved slowly forwards, steering gently between all the bobbing yachts anchored in the harbour, before picking up speed and swerving towards the river mouth and the rocky headland jutting into the sea just beyond.

Mr Rattacheck saw me staring at the starter button and read my mind. He took the key ring he'd collected earlier from his pocket. 'This has an electronic fob attached. So long as it's inside the boat, it will activate the engine. No keys required. This one on the key ring is to the boathouse with the red doors over there on the beach. That's where I keep this baby locked safely away at night.'

His hand gently slid a throttle lever very slightly and we instantly gained speed. With open water ahead, he could coolly turn and talk to us while keeping one hand on the steering wheel. 'I'll take you just round the headland into the tiny Smuggler's Cove first. Sometimes there are seals round there where it's quiet.'

The only way down to the beach in the cove was through a long tunnel from an inn tucked in to the cliffs. I'd once gone with Mum down the spooky passages through the rocks called 'Smuggler's Tunnel'. It was used by smugglers long ago at night to smuggle brandy and lace from France up to the inn. The winding steps and twisty tunnel is open to the public a few times a year for ghost tours, as it's meant to be haunted by the smugglers who got hacked down by customs officers with bayonets. Most of the time the cove is deserted and only accessible by boat.

The Cooper's Inn at the end of the tunnel opens on some weekends, but it's so dark and spooky that after we ate there once, Mum said 'never again'.

As we turned into the cove, I could see why this was

a perfect spot for smuggling goods ashore without being seen from anywhere. Mr Rattacheck peered around through binoculars. 'It looks like the seals are on holiday. We may see dolphins later. You can see cormorants on those rocks and oyster catchers on the cliffs. Is there anywhere you want to go from here?'

I asked, 'Can we go to the bay below the caravan park? I'd like to see if my stones are still standing.'

'My pleasure. You'd better hold on to your hats. The tide is coming in and where it meets the current of the river, it could be choppy. Fasten seat belts.'

Suddenly the boat leapt from the water and seemed to fly over the waves. A cloud of spray flew over us as we bounced across the sea, the speed pushing us back into our seats and the wind stinging our eyes. It was fantastic.

Skimming over the choppier water at the river mouth, we leapt from one wave to the next. Each time we slapped down, a spew of foam sprayed us. I got drenched, but it was so warm I didn't care. We just squealed and high-fived our way across the gleaming sea, unable to believe this was real.

The boat sped round the cliffs of the next headland and turned in a wide arc towards the shore. The high rusty-red cliffs stretched up ahead of us and on the top I could see a couple of caravans perched between trees, where a wisp of smoke rose into a cloudless sky. As the boat swept round, churning the sea fluorescent white behind us, we slowed and drifted close to the beach. Only a few people were paddling or swimming and I could see clearly that some of my stones were still balancing in their fragile towers, although they didn't look so impressive from a distance.

A woman walking with a dog waved to us and Mr Rattacheck waved back, shouting to her. 'Glad to see you're back!'

'You seem to know everyone round here,' Sophie said to him.

'Liz works for me,' he answered, still waving. 'She and Bryn live up in that caravan on the left. They manage the caravan park for me. It's good to know she's safe and well.'

Sophie gave me one of her looks before saying to him, 'I'd heard that Liz Baker went missing and that Bryn Griffiths had done something horrible to her.'

'Not Bryn,' he answered. 'He might be a rough diamond at times but he wouldn't harm Liz. In fact, he was really upset last weekend that she might have been swept out to sea. I lent him this boat so he could go out and search for her. I have to say, I feared the worst when I heard the lunchtime news today.'

We both watched and waited, wondering whatever he was going to say next.

'This morning they found a woman's body on the beach, further down the coast.'

NINE

Merlin darted across the room before pouncing on a ping-pong ball and dabbing it back to me. I picked him up, held him in my arms and stood at the window, looking down at Sophie's gran pegging out washing in the garden. I could feel Merlin purring, his whole body vibrating as he nuzzled into me and licked my chin. I told him how I'd soon be taking him home with me and that we'd be friends for life.

Sophie and I spent Saturday morning sorting out all the stuff to sell in our shop that I'd named '**Fin**tasticly **Soph**isticated', which we had to explain to her gran, who didn't seem impressed. We showed her all the pictures of our boat trip, from checked yachting shoes to me getting soaked by a freak wave. She still didn't seem impressed – but the final straw came when the local paper arrived and she got really huffy at being upstaged by me, as she hardly got a mention. There was a cheesy photo of me holding Merlin, standing next to Mr Rattacheck. The headline said *Stone Boy Rocks!* It showed a close-up of one of my cards and made it seem like I was some kind of superhero, saving a half-dead kitten by single-handedly raising a fortune and rushing him to the vet in the nick of time. It made it look like I'd begged Mr Rattacheck to help and he'd come parachuting in to save the day. It was all a lot of rubbish, but I guess deep down I felt chuffed that my cards were getting a mention. Sophie laughed at the bit that described me as a 'Mini-Enterprise Entrepreneur', which was a bit of a joke as I didn't have a clue what one of those was.

We both had another reason to take a close look at the newspaper. It had a report of the incident we wanted to know about. The article didn't give us much more information than what we'd found online the night before.

BODY FOUND ON BEACH

Police officers were called to Redsands Bay just before 10:00 on Friday morning by a man walking his dog, who reported the discovery of a body in a rock pool at low tide. A police cordon is in place on the beach and an investigation is under way. The death is currently being treated as unexplained and the body, believed to be that of a young woman, has not yet been identified.

'It could be anyone,' I suggested. 'We'll never know if it's anything to do with Operation BHM. Probably just a coincidence.'

'Unless the poor woman turns out to be a certain Ella Brookes,' Sophie said. I did a quick search online and announced, 'Redsands Bay is miles up the coast. I don't think there's a connection.'

'All will be revealed in time,' Sophie added. 'Maybe when Lian arrives tomorrow she'll tell us stuff, and then we can plan our investigation, my dear Watson.'

I just smiled. I wasn't sure about this anymore.

We caught a bus to the garden centre and I was convinced people were staring at me, now I was in the paper. I told Sophie it was a strain being a celebrity, so she told me to put a paper bag over my head and forget it. In a way I did feel important, as her gran had given us both special ID passes so we could bring back money from the collecting boxes at the garden centre. It was great to wave them at a woman behind a counter and then be taken into a back office and given biscuits before we sorted the coins into bags. It was just as I was opening up the back of a collecting dog statue in the café that I was aware of someone running towards me with her arms open. For a split second I thought I was being robbed by a mad woman, but then I saw it was Mrs Holmes.

'Fin, my love – fancy seeing you here, helping out like this. How lovely to see you. Are you having a good holiday? Hey, hold on, where are they?'

I was so stunned to see her, I was speechless.

'Yes, I'm not surprised you've lost your tongue, young man,' she went on, wagging her finger. 'Does Mum know you haven't got them?'

I don't know what came over me at that moment, it was really weird. In fact, it was more than that. Just the mention of Mum made me think of how I'd left her that morning. She'd been crying in the garden and I remembered how, for the first time when I glanced back at her as I'd waved goodbye, she'd looked so vulnerable and dependent on me. That image in my head suddenly made the tears rise in my eyes and I just couldn't stop them streaming down my face. Mrs Holmes looked horrified.

'Fin, darling, whatever's the matter? I'm only teasing. What's wrong, love?'

I felt such a fool – this had never happened to me before. I tried to speak, but the words got stuck and I just stood there and blubbed in the middle of a crowded café, with Mrs Holmes giving me a big hug and trying to dry my eyes.

'I'm sorry,' I managed to splutter eventually. 'It's just that Mum's very ill and I'm so worried about her. You just reminded me, that's all. Sorry, miss.'

'Sweetheart,' she said, still hugging me, 'you poor love. Come on, let's have a drink, a chunk of carrot cake and a little chat. I had no idea about your mum. Let's go over there and sit by the window and I'll see what I can do.'

As if I wasn't embarrassed enough by my outburst, Sophie then appeared and saw the state of me. Mrs Holmes gave her a big hug (she hugs everyone) and they were soon gabbling away – presumably about me. Then, to cap it all, a woman in the queue pointed at me as I was dabbing my eyes and shouted, 'Ooh look, it's that lad in the paper – the one who gets stoned.'

Everyone stared as I skulked away to a table and sat with my head in my hands. I wasn't just mortified – I was actually really scared at how I'd lost it without any warning. I just didn't know what had come over me and it was so weird. It was as if Mrs Holmes had knocked against my safety valve and suddenly released the pressure bubbling inside me.

Mrs Holmes was brilliant, as always. She could see I was a hopeless wreck and how I was totally freaked out by my own reaction.

'It's all right, Fin. It's quite normal for our feelings to take us over and upset us now and again. It's what being a teenager is all about.'

'Yeah,' I sniffed. 'The trouble is, I'm still thirteen. I didn't expect this stuff to happen till Thursday, when I hit the big one-four.'

She smiled and put her hand on my arm, 'Blame the hormones, Fin. They can play havoc with emotions. I've been blaming mine for the last fifty years.'

Sophie couldn't resist joining in. 'Join the club. For someone who tries to be balanced and in control, I'm always upsetting myself about silly stuff.'

I knew she was trying to make me feel better, but that set me off again.

'This isn't silly stuff,' I spluttered. 'I think my mum's dying.'

As soon as I said it, I wished I hadn't. Now Sophie and Mrs Holmes began looking awkward and watery-eyed. I didn't want to talk about it, but Mrs Holmes has the knack of making anyone open up and tell it as it is. So that's what I did between mouthfuls of carrot cake in the middle of the garden centre café. I told her all about Mum going into hospital the next day.

Mrs Homes listened in her usual patient way before touching my hand. 'You must concentrate on what I'm saying, Fin. I know I'm not your teacher anymore, but I want you to promise to keep in touch. You can email me at any time.' She gave me her card. 'I mean it.'

'Thanks, Miss.'

'I'm not *Miss* anymore, am I? You can call me June, if you like. Do you know, I'm delighted you two are friends. I didn't even know you knew each other. To be honest, and I know I'm not supposed to say this, as teachers aren't meant to have favourites … you two were my stars. I loved teaching you both. And the thing is, Fin, you might sometimes need an old woman like me to chat to now and again. If ever I can do anything to help while Mum's in hospital, you must ask. I'm sure Sophie and her gran will keep an eye on you, but never be afraid to scream for help. I know you're an independent young man with a strong will and a sharp brain, but sometimes you need to admit you need to communicate what's going on in that little head of yours. And you know what I'm like at making you communicate properly, eh? I'll never stop nagging you to use all those skills I've tried to teach you. Keep those eyes and hands tuned-in and never give up, because you've got what it takes, Fin. Trust me.'

I nodded feebly, then took myself off to clean up my face from the after-effects of cake smeared with tears. Then, with my rucksack full of coins, I pushed Sophie back to the bus stop, where she had to argue with the driver to let us on the bus because it was nearly full and her chair would take up too much room. She said something about human rights and being mayor one day – and amazingly we were allowed on the bus with no more fuss.

When we got back, we re-counted and bagged up all the loose change we'd collected from the garden centre.

'You had over one hundred and fifty pounds in your rucksack,' Sophie said. 'We could have been kidnapped. Then again, who'd take us two on?'

'Just the wonderful Mrs Holmes,' I answered.

'Ah yes, Holmes to the rescue again, my dear Watson. In fact, it's time for more detective work. Geoff the fish man is outside and I've got questions.' She grabbed her sticks and rushed to the front door, calling after Geoff, who was returning to his van. 'Geoff, can I ask a quick question?'

'And what would that be, Soph? I bet it's nothing to do with the price of fish.'

'It's about that body at Redsands Bay yesterday. Do you know anything?'

'Can't say I do. The coastguard told me about it. They've yet to identify her. As far as I know it's nothing suspicious. Poor woman probably fell off a cliff into the sea. It happens from time to time. I've found a few now and again.'

I was watching Sophie's every word and move. 'Could the body have been in the sea for a week, do you think? I mean, wouldn't it rot much?'

'The sea can preserve really well,' he answered. 'Without being too gruesome, I once hauled up a young lad in my nets who'd been surfing but got swept away and drowned. In his wet suit in the cold water he looked as good as new, even though he'd been dead a few weeks. Mind you, I've known bodies found in shallow water just outside the harbour to be nibbled to bits by crabs and all sorts in no time. Not a pretty sight, I can tell you.'

We both pulled horrific faces, but only Sophie had the courage to ask the next question. 'Redsands Bay is a long way from here, right?'

'Over fifty miles, I guess.'

'Is it possible, do you think, for a body to drift that far from here in a few days?'

Geoff raised his eyebrows. 'Now you're asking. The answer is, "it all depends". The sea is a complex system of winds, tides, currents, weather, air pressure and all sorts. I've known flotsam to travel getting on for fifty miles in a day. Other times it goes nowhere. The main long-shore drift along this coast from here is in the direction of Redsands Bay, so it's perfectly possible, I guess.'

'So if I dropped a ball into the sea off the cliff here, could it end up fifty miles away in a week?' I chipped in.

'Unlikely, son. Not so close to shore. Further out maybe. There's a fair pull eastwards just offshore at this time of year and in the winds we've had lately. To be honest, I've learned never to be surprised by anything the sea does – with a ball, a body, a boat or a dirty great basking shark for that matter. I saw one of those only yesterday just offshore. This job's always full of surprises – like customers who don't let me get on – I must skedaddle, Sophie, before the ice melts in this heat ... ' He jumped into the driver's seat and sped off, leaving Sophie and me looking at one another with a look that said, 'It could be possible.' Then again, what we were thinking seemed highly unlikely.

We went back indoors to give Merlin the last of his tablets, play another game of ping-pong with him, then clean out all the cats in the garage before feeding time. By the time I got home in the evening I was shattered, but delighted to see Uncle Calvin's car wasn't in our road. I was amazed to see Mum icing a cake in the kitchen and with make-up on.

'I've made you a birthday cake, Fin. It can go in the freezer for Thursday. And I've decided to take you out somewhere tonight for a nice meal. I could do with going out with a young man, so get in the shower, smarten yourself up and it's a night on the town for us. It's about time I showed my blood cells who's boss.'

'Let me pay, Mum. I've got some money hidden away in my drawer.'

'I'll hear no such thing, Fin. This is a birthday treat and

we'll go wherever you like. My latest blood transfusion has given me a new lease of life, so let's make hay while the sun shines. Where do you fancy eating?'

I didn't need to think for long. 'Well, I've set foot in one place that might be worth a look. Now that I'm a celebrity and mix with rich businessmen, how about dining at one of my clients' establishments?'

'Sorry, love – you've lost me.'

'Let's try The Actor's Creak in town. I happen to know the boss.'

By the time we walked into town, the sky was orange and the sun bright red. There was a strong breeze off the sea and it was high tide, so waves were splashing over the sea wall.

'How about a walk along the prom to see if we can dodge the waves? I bet it's you who gets soaked,' Mum laughed.

'Yeah, I'm up for it,' I answered. I knew she was making a real effort to be like her old self for our last evening together. I didn't think it was just for my benefit, but she was doing this for herself too – something to feed on in the uncertain days ahead.

We weren't the only people trying our luck playing Russian roulette with the sea or, as Mum called it, running the wave-gauntlet (whatever that meant).

A few splats landed right near us as a sudden shower sprayed over the railings. The promenade was speckled with damp patches as far ahead as the start of the cliff road, rising beyond the waves' reach.

'I'll go first,' Mum giggled, just like her old self. 'Give me a head start of a few metres, then you follow behind at the same pace, keeping a steady distance. The winner is the driest when we get to that bench on the cliff road. No running or dodging. Stiff upper lip if you get splattered. Good luck.'

She turned, took a deep breath, and began marching slowly, swinging her arms like a soldier. After about ten metres she turned to signal that I should follow. She gave a salute and, in that second, the path right behind her got a soaking. Surprisingly, only a few splashes caught the back of her legs. We both laughed, then I set off slowly, keeping my eyes fixed on Mum's feet walking ahead of me. When I reached the patch that just got hit, I assumed (like lightning supposedly not striking the same spot twice) another wave right there wouldn't happen. I was wrong and I got soaked by a real belter. Mum took one look at me and almost dropped to her knees with laughing. My hair and face were sopping. People stared at us as if we were mad.

In the warm breeze my face and shoulders were already drying by the time we'd pulled ourselves together. Further ahead, the pounding waves were flying over the steps leading down to the beach and the spray even reached the flowerbeds along the seafront. Where sunlight caught the fine mist, a tiny rainbow hung in the air in front of us. Mum marched on, with me following behind – each of us getting near misses. She was in full stride just past halfway when a massive wave crashed into the wall, bounced back and caught the next wave rolling in. The sea exploded in shooting showers of foam, one of them catching Mum smack in the back. Her red top was drenched, the dark splatters down her back looking like she'd been peppered by a machine gun. Once more we stopped to laugh helplessly before striding onwards to the safety of the higher path ahead.

When Mum arrived at the bench, she stood on it and waved triumphantly, then clapped as I emerged through the misty spray unscathed. We sat on the bench giggling and chatting in that warm sea breeze, with the orange light of sunset on our faces, and I so wished I could bottle that moment. It felt so good to be out there and it seemed none of our worries had made it across the 'path of a hundred splats' as Mum called it. She put her arm round my shoulders and said cheerfully, 'Do you know what, Fin? I reckon that little experience bodes well for you and me. Maybe we're lucky after all and from here on things will be fine. That walk was like the journey of our lives. You got sloshed very early on and I got a pounding half way through, but we carried on regardless and made it safely through. Now we're as dry as a bone and can look back with a radiant smile. Maybe things are going to work out okay after all.'

Walking through the revolving doors of The Actor's Creak, we were both in high spirits and hungry. We were greeted by a dark-skinned man in a shiny waistcoat, the sort of waiter that makes Mum swoon. He spoke to her, then she turned to me with a shrug and told me they had no tables. I don't know what came over me, but I stepped forward and said, 'Excuse me, I was here yesterday with Mr Rattacheck. He took me out on his boat. Those are my cards he's selling at the desk. He's a friend.'

'One moment, sir,' he said and went away, leaving Mum and me staring at each other, grinning. I had never been called 'sir' before in my life. When he returned he led us to a small table by a stage where a band was playing.

'We can squeeze you in here but I'm afraid it's a bit loud next to the jazz band.' Mum didn't hear him above the noise, but I just mouthed to him, 'That's no problem for me.'

He handed us menus and went away. Mum gave a big 'thumbs-up'.

'Well done, Fin. Great jazz, a dishy waiter and a companion with influence. What could be better? It's a bit classy here, but why not? It's not every week you become fourteen, Fin. I can't believe my little boy is growing up so fast.'

The waiter returned. 'Sorry to keep you. Can I get you some drinks? Mr Rattacheck says the drinks are on him. He apologises for not coming over to see you but we're very busy tonight. We are two waitresses short.'

'Can't you get taller ones?' I grinned. He didn't smile but said something about unreliable staff. What he said next really made me take notice.

'The trouble is,' he went on, 'Cheri, our front-of-house manager, broke her ankle this morning and Ella's been off for a week.'

'Sorry, what did you say?' I asked. 'Did you say Ella?'

'Yes, one of our star waitresses. No one seems to know where she went off to. She hadn't been here long, either. That's the trouble here, no one stays long.'

'Not Ella Brookes, by any chance?'

'I think that's her name, yes. Lovely girl. She just didn't turn up for work on Monday. She didn't even let us know. It's not easy to get staff who are committed – like me! Anyway, are you ready to order?'

I wasn't, actually. I needed to text Sophie there and then with the ground-breaking news.

TEN

After our fun time out on Saturday night, the next morning was really dismal. It wasn't just down to the heavy mist sweeping in off the sea, but indoors the cloud was hanging over us, too. As Mum packed for going off to hospital, she'd lost all her sparkle from the night before. I was also feeling gloomy at the thought of the Uncle Calvin cloud already rumbling its way down the motorway. Mum blamed her dark mood on a terrible headache caused by the loud band at The Actor's Creak, as well as all the thunder in the night.

'You're lucky, Fin – such things don't bother you.'

'It might be more to do with the free red wine you had last night,' I joked.

She didn't say anything, but I guess we both feared her 'bad head days', as she called them, were caused by something more sinister. She was becoming more anxious as the time approached for Uncle Calvin to take her off to hospital, so I tried to keep out of the way in the background. Sophie kept texting to tell me to meet at her gran's, which she now called HQ, but that would have to wait till I'd spent time with Mum and said our goodbyes.

By midday, as the sky brightened, so did Mum, and I waited to be summoned for one of her little chats, when I knew I'd have to promise to pay full attention and do as I was told. Sure enough, she switched on the bright light in the kitchen and shut the window blind, which was the sign for sitting at the table for a 'board meeting' as she always called our chats. I called them interrogations, but she insisted it helped communication when clear-speaking was necessary. I told her that's what the Gestapo said, but she attacked me with a broom – in a motherly way, rather than a secret police kind of way. I sat and waited for her to begin.

'Fin, I know I'm a bit of a control freak and like to have things organised for us both, but I realise I need to back off a bit, especially as you're about to hit a big birthday. The thing is, I've got to learn that I'm just not in control over the next weeks. That's dead scary and I know I'll hate it. But love, please don't you worry about me. I want you to enjoy your holiday and birthday and everything. I'm so glad you've got Sophie and her gran to go to and, even though you don't get on that great with Uncle Calvin, it's good of him and Jasmine to come here to house-sit for me. I don't expect you to spend all your time with them, but just be friendly and polite, do you understand?'

'Yes, Mum. I'll be as good as gold. I'll miss you loads, but you mustn't worry about me. I'll come and see you in hospital as soon as they let visitors in, but until then keep emailing messages.'

'I'll do better than that,' she said. 'I've decided to set up a blog. Some of my friends want me to keep them posted, so I thought I'd go public with what they're doing to me – in the hope it will encourage people to give blood and donate stem cells – not just for me but for hospitals round the country. I'm really glad I used to give blood when I was younger, it's so important.'

I told her I'd definitely become a donor the day I hit eighteen. 'Just four more years!'

She suddenly looked terrified. 'Oh, Fin – I'm so scared I won't be there for you ... '

I could see she was getting upset again, so I quickly handed her a card I'd made. It wasn't like all my others. This was special – personal. I told her to open it when she woke the next morning, as I knew we'd both end up crying if we didn't change the subject, so I just blurted, 'Would you let me have a kitten?'

She smiled. 'I never say "never", Fin. Maybe not just now, but when I come home again I might be persuaded – if all goes well.'

'I'll take that as a sort of "yes", then.'

'We'll see. Tell you what, let's get a spot of lunch. Calvin will join us for a bite and then they'll take me to the hospital. No doubt you've got some plans for this afternoon?'

I told her I was seeing Sophie and meeting a friend of the missing waitress.

'That's nice, love.' I could tell she hadn't even heard what I said. Then again, I guessed she had more pressing things on her mind.

'Are you okay?' Sophie asked me, while I dragged a piece of string across Merlin's dozing, twitching body.

'It was tough saying goodbye to Mum, but we just about coped. It was far tougher saying hello to Uncle Calvin. I don't think I said anything to Jasmine, as she ignores me. I think she sees me as some sort of freak of nature. Come to think of it, that's what I see her as. Since she freaked me out at New Year by sleeping naked in our bathroom, I can't look at her now without needing therapy and a course of treatment with a trained counsellor.'

Suddenly Merlin sprang and decided that attacking my fingers was more fun than string. I laughed as he scampered off mischievously, while Sophie grabbed her phone. 'It's Lian. She's just getting a taxi from the station. I hope she likes lemon drizzle. Gran's made a cake specially.'

We went downstairs into what was their back room, where a little table was set with a lace cloth and a cake stand with all sorts of little cakes on doilies. Beside it was the famous lemon drizzle.

'I do think it's important to have a proper Sunday afternoon tea,' Mrs Boughtwood announced. 'Just ignore the smell of fish seeping from the steamy walls. It's an occupational hazard, I'm afraid. Sorry to hear about your mother, Finley. Feel free to come and have meals here at any time. It won't always be fish, I promise you. Once your shop starts tomorrow you'll be a member of the team here, so come and go as you like. Was that the doorbell? I expect your visitor has arrived – I'll show her in and leave you to it.'

'I've got no idea what to expect,' Sophie said. 'Lian seemed nice on the phone, but … ' Before she could finish speaking, it was as if a whirlwind had swept into the room. A tiny young woman with short black bristly hair and deep brown eyes, lots of dangly jewellery, bright yellow top and shorts, and sparkly pink shoes hugged us like we were long-lost friends and spoke so fast I could hardly keep up. She was bubbling and fizzing with energy.

'I'm so glad you called me, you don't know how relieved I was to get your message. I feel so guilty, too, for not getting in touch with Ella for so long. I'd been worried about her for a few days when she wasn't answering her phone but then I thought she probably lost it – I'm always losing my phone. But hey, you guys, tell me how you know the lovely Ella. I was hoping she might be here – I'd love to see her if you know where she is.'

'One thing at a time,' Sophie began. 'I explained on the phone that we haven't actually met her, but we know she was staying somewhere nearby. Fin found her wallet and necklace, maybe her sandal and bag on the beach. We started doing some detective work and you're one of her contacts, so we thought you should know what we fear might have happened.'

'Fear? Why? What happened? You didn't tell me anything happened.' She sat down beside me and looked worried, so I just said, 'I found out last night that Ella was a waitress in town at a place called The Actor's Creak, but she left work a week ago without telling anyone or without giving a new address.'

'Just like Ella! So where's her old address?' She was already scribbling in a small notebook.

'We don't know. But the thing is … a body of a woman has just been found along the coast.'

'No!' she slapped her hand to her mouth. 'What do the police say?'

Sophie explained about the hand on the beach, the police not being particularly concerned, and of my suspicions about Bryn Griffiths.

'So her last tweet,' Lian said, about being "on a mission" and "if I disappear" must have been serious. I assumed the poem she posted was just one of her many little songs she writes that I don't always get. I didn't really take it seriously. Maybe she was on some undercover work.'

'A spy?' My voice must have sounded so shocked and squeaky that they both laughed.

'Not a spy, exactly.' Lian looked directly at me and took a deep breath – probably her first intake of air since she'd burst in. 'Let me explain. My parents are Chinese and they sent me to Britain for my education. When I went to uni I met Ella, where we both studied Journalism and Media and became great friends. When we left we shared a flat for a few months in Manchester, where we did freelance stuff at Media City. When I got a job with the BBC in Glasgow, Ella decided to try her hand working for herself in investigative journalism. She's always been on a mission to help the underdog by exposing any dirty deeds of bigwigs in power. I know she was following one or two leads and working on a piece for *Watchdog* on TV before she decided to take a summer break – "somewhere by the sea" is all she told me.'

Sophie was nodding furiously and hanging on Lian's every word. 'So when did you last see her?' she asked.

Once more Lian launched into a gabbling monologue, waving her hands and bracelets all over the place. 'Back in June, when we arranged to meet up for her birthday in September. I'm ashamed to say I've been so busy that I've not emailed her or phoned for a few weeks. Then, when you contacted me and said she was here and you'd found her necklace, that was a great excuse for me to take a break and come to find out more and hopefully catch up with her, seeing as I wasn't getting any replies from my calls to her. I do hope she's okay. We'll have to check out about the body they found, but I daren't think about it. I guess I ought to find out if Ella knew this Bryn person you mentioned.'

'Why not just send out a message on social media asking if anyone knows where Ella Brookes is?' I suggested.

'I don't think so,' Lian answered immediately, looking very serious. 'I wouldn't want her family to know we're worried about her – it's a long story, but her younger sister and parents live in Canada. They don't have much to do with her as they think she's a bit of a rebel. One whiff that Ella could be in trouble and they'd become unbearable. And besides, if the world knows she's missing, that could alert all sorts of undesirables and nutters. The first rule when starting an investigation is to keep your powder dry by not letting people know what you're doing. Ella's brilliant at that, and at keeping everything secret until the very end. She's very professional. Let's just hope she's on the trail of a really good story and she's lying low somewhere. She's done it before. I wouldn't be surprised if she split up with her latest boyfriend and needed space – time away off the radar to clear her head with sea air and time by herself – that's just like her.'

Sophie looked at Ella's Facebook page on her phone. 'She looks so pretty and happy in her photos, and lists all sorts of "likes".'

'One of Ella's things is word puzzles like Scrabble and stuff,' Lian went on. 'I'm always telling her that's a bit nerdy, but I wouldn't be surprised she's got a room around here for the week and she's just lying on the beach with a glass of fizz and a book of crosswords. That would be just up her street.'

'Just up mine, too,' Sophie said. 'Ella sounds really cool. I do hope we can find her and she's all right.'

Lian took out her own phone. 'I've got some great pictures of her on here. Here she's wearing that bracelet with matching earrings I gave her. I'm going to do all I can to find her – I'm going to get on the case straight away. Once I've dropped off my suitcase at the B and B I've booked for the next couple of nights, I reckon my first job is to go to where Ella was a waitress and ask a few questions.' She looked at her notebook. 'The Actor's Creak. Then, if I can find out where she was staying, I'll start snooping around. Once I get some hard facts, we'll be able to find out if Ella's okay or … ' She paused before giving a sigh, 'or whether I have to go to the police. Either way, I shan't give up. Once I get on a case I'm like a rottweiler with a bone.'

'Or me with a slice of lemon drizzle,' Sophie said. 'Anyone for cake?'

By the time Lian had finished showing us pictures of Ella and planning her next moves, the cake had virtually disappeared.

When I got home, the dreaded red car was back outside our gate. I'd hoped they might still be out or gone to the pub. As soon as I walked indoors I was in a fug of cigarette smoke, burnt chips and greasy steam wafting from the kitchen.

'Hello, Uncle Calvin,' I said, as cheerfully as I could. He was slouched over the sofa, watching TV alone.

'Shsh, Jasmine's having a rest in the bedroom,' he said, without taking his eyes off the screen. 'When she's up, we want a word with you, seeing as we're now in charge here.'

I tried to smile. 'Was Mum okay?'

'What do you think?' he snapped. 'If she was okay she wouldn't be in hospital, would she? Blockhead.'

With Mum out of the way, this was his golden opportunity to behave like his true self. He could now begin to show what he really thought of me, with no one to keep the peace.

'That's not what I meant,' I said softly. 'I was asking if you got there okay and if she was all right with her room and everything.'

'We didn't hang about, not with the price of parking. We left her in the waiting room. I don't do hospitals. They give Jasmine the jitters, too. Oh, and those flowers you gave your mum – Jasmine kept them. No flowers allowed in your mum's room.'

I didn't say anything but turned and walked away. He shouted after me but I didn't go back. So much for keeping quiet to avoid disturbing his precious Jasmine, I thought, as I went to my bedroom to get out of the way. Once inside, I immediately sensed they'd been there. Stuff on my table had been moved. Liking a tidy bedroom with everything in its own place, I could see my things had definitely been disturbed. I seethed with far more than anger. My fingers were trembling, my head was spinning and I felt sick inside. It was like I was losing control again, just as I did at the garden centre. It was scary – but I was sure this was nothing to do with hormones. It was a mix of rage and fear. Maybe the Intermittent Explosive Disorder gene was kicking in. I was determined to strike back, but not yet – when I was in more of a mood for a fight.

I moved a chair against the door to wedge the handle and to barricade myself inside. For the first time in my life, I felt frightened being in my own bedroom and I knew without doubt the next day was bound to get far worse.

ELEVEN

There was no sign of life when I got up on Monday morning. Uncle Calvin had told me he usually stayed in bed till late, so I left before anyone else was up. After all, I didn't have time to waste – I had a shop to set up.

By the time I arrived in Braxted Avenue with another bagful of cards, the sun was beating down, a warm breeze stirred the trees and people were out watering their gardens. Mrs Boughtwood was stretching up to her hanging baskets with a leaking watering can.

'Talk about a heatwave,' she moaned. 'That thunder the other night was no good at bringing rain. There's already talk of a hosepipe ban.'

'Good weather means good profits for our shop, I reckon,' I said.

'We'll soon see. I've put some folded picnic tables in

the hall, so just open up the front gates and set them up right across the drive. I've also got bunting to drape across and a blackboard on an easel to announce special offers. There's a tin of cash for a float, so there's all you need. Sophie is just putting the price tags on my china vases.'

I wasn't ready for her next question, asked with one of her fixed grins.

'Did you ask your mother if you can have the kitten?'

'Merlin? Yes.' I meant that I had asked.

'Good, that's settled, then. You can take him home this evening. He's better now, we need the spare room and I know you'll look after him well.'

I tried to explain. 'I'd love to have him, but I'm not sure … '

'How to get him home? No problem, you can borrow a cat basket. You can have some tins of food that he's used to. That's marvellous – another abandoned animal successfully homed.'

I didn't argue. I longed to have someone at home to talk to and Merlin was such a great little character that I'd be able to chat to him in our secret den.

Passers-by soon stopped to look at what we were selling. My packs of cards and envelopes 'at knock-down prices' sold like hot cakes. I recorded each sale in a book so I could work out how much to give to Guide Dogs and how much I'd keep. By midday Sophie and I were having a great time and selling all kinds of junk. I'd made a banner saying 'Fintasticly Sophisticated' which we had to keep explaining till Sophie had the bright idea of wearing name badges. Then lots of people thought it was a cool name and the money came rolling in, while we just sat there in the sun with iced drinks.

Lian greeted us enthusiastically, just as I was selling a batch of old comics. She sat with us and told us what she'd found out that morning.

'First of all, no one has a clue why Ella went off at the end of her shift the Sunday evening a week ago. She left no forwarding address and has two weeks' pay owed to her. But guess what? They've given me her job! I start tomorrow, so I'll be able to do a bit of digging around by talking to the staff.'

Sophie gave her high-fives and a hug. 'Did you find out where Ella was staying?'

'I did. Number fifty-two Clifftop Caravan Park. Not only that, I went there and used my charms on Bryn Griffiths.'

I didn't like the thought of that. 'I hope he didn't spit at you,' I said.

'I think I found him in a good mood, because I'll be renting the very same caravan as Ella. I didn't let on that I know her, but he kept on about the last occupant who'd cleared out all her stuff and left in a hurry. He didn't seem to know much about her other than her name and that she owed him rent. So once I get in there, I'm going to have a thorough search. If I know Ella, she'd have left one or two clues behind.'

'That's brilliant,' Sophie said. 'A good day's work all round. We've just made our first hundred pounds.'

I arrived home with Merlin trying to scratch my fingers through the basket. Thankfully no one was around, so I could get to the shed without being seen. I let him explore his new surroundings – a bit nervously at first, but he was soon pouncing on a feather, dabbing at cobwebs and chasing spiders. I fed him, sat beside him and read Mum's texts, sent her a message then played with him till he was ready to curl up in his bed. Eventually I left him in his new home and went indoors to check out Mum's first blog entry.

> Monday 5pm
> I've only been here 24 hours and already it feels like forever! After all the checks and scans, I've just had my first dose of chemo. This will go on for eight days while I have to stay in my room with one window and a delightful view of a brick wall. Staff and I have to wear face masks because my immune system is about to do a nosedive even more. I'm not sure what to expect exactly as they tell me different people react differently. It's most likely I will lose my hair, but I get a wig. How about frizzy blonde or red spikes?
>
> I've got loads of pills to take and the nurses have to keep waking me up to give them to me. So far the food is OK and I've still got an appetite – until my taste-buds go on strike or shrivel up, or whatever they do. More on that subject tomorrow.
>
> My consultant came to see me today.

Basically, everything now depends on them finding a suitable bone marrow donor. The one they'd lined up didn't work out, for some reason. That's a real blow. I'd assumed they'd just put my details into a database and up would pop another match. So far there isn't one – so if anyone out there fancies giving a quick saliva sample to see if you can help me, please get in touch.

More news tomorrow, folks!

I sat for a long time reading her words over and over again. I couldn't wait to talk to her later when we planned to Skype. In the meantime, I had to make do with talking to her photo I now kept by my bed.

When I went to the kitchen to put the kettle on, I was gutted to see Jasmine with her head in the fridge. Her gigantic butt blotted out the fridge light like a total eclipse of the sun. Uncle Calvin slouched in a chair with a box of bottles and a scowl that could turn the steam from the kettle to ice.

'Where have you been?' he snapped.

'I've been running a front gate-sale in town to make money for guide dogs.'

'Have you, now? I'm sure your granddad would be mighty impressed. Trouble is, I'm not.'

'The kettle's on – cup of tea anyone?' I asked cheerily, although I already sensed trouble. Suddenly he slammed his fist on the kitchen table. 'Sit down and pay attention. We've got straight talking to do.'

I did as he said, without daring to argue, and saw Jasmine turn to watch, smiling as if she was ready for some carefully rehearsed entertainment.

'How do you mean?' I asked.

'I'm in charge of you now, Fin. You do as I say from now on. I'm your official guardian while your mum's in hospital. We've signed to say so. Your mum agreed.'

'Signed?' I was confused.

'Exactly. I wanted it all done properly. Then we know where we stand. Then the child benefit comes to me direct.'

'But Mum left you money in the fruit bowl for food and stuff.' She'd told me that.

'Well, it's not enough.'

Jasmine chipped in next. 'Not enough to keep a fly alive. We like to eat well, don't we, Cal? We have high standards in the cuisine department. We like our liquid refreshment too.' She laughed and I couldn't stop myself blurting, 'So is that why you've been in my room? Looking for cash, were you?'

I wasn't prepared for his answer. In fact, I'd expected him to get in a strop. Instead, he sat back and nodded. 'So you noticed,' he smirked. 'I was going to tell you, anyway. As your guardian, I need to make sure I take my responsibilities seriously. That's why I'm keeping your two hundred quid safe for you. I found it rolled up in your drawer. It's the least I can do in my new important role *in loco parentis*.'

'You can't do that!' I stood up and I, too, thumped my fist on the table, making all the spoons jump and fall to the floor.

Jasmine came over and put her face right up to mine, nose to nose. 'You can't stop him, love. Cal is like your own father now – except he's a real man. You're still only thirteen, pet. By law, you have to obey your legal guardian. If you want to buy anything, you just ask Cal and he'll make a decision if you can have it. He must determine exactly what's in your best interests. Simple. That's how proper fathers work. Not that you've ever had one of those.'

I couldn't speak. I could hardly breathe. My insides felt like they were about to explode. What made it worse, and they knew it, was that they were smiling smugly all the time. He leaned back in his chair and said, 'You see, Fin, although I love my sister to bits, she's been a crap wife and mother. She's spoilt you rotten and that's why you've turned out like this. You couldn't help your unfortunate start in life, but ever since you've cunningly wound her and my dad round your little finger and got everything you want. Well, that's about to change, as I consider it my responsibility to make you toe the line and learn some lessons of life. The first is that you stop using this place like a hotel, coming and going as you please without asking permission. You can hand over your front door key for a start.'

Jasmine took over next, just as if they were following a script. 'And there's no use going crying to your mother, because you can't. One: she's ill and she'll get worse if you upset her. Two: Uncle Calvin will be in charge of all your online activity from now on. He'll need to check your emails to approve everything and make sure you're not going on any inappropriate websites. There's no telling what filth you're used to watching.'

'Not as much as you though, Jas!' They both rocked laughing and that's when I erupted. I'm not sure what I actually shouted, but I know it involved a gross description of the filthiest stuff I'd ever had to experience – namely her naked anatomy rolling on our bathroom floor like a pregnant hippo. That wiped the smiles off their faces. In fact, her face puffed up even more than ever, her neck turned scarlet and her eyes looked like they were about to swivel, pop out of their sockets and burst.

'Tell him, Cal!' she screamed.

He took a lunge at me but I dodged his fist, swore and ran to my room. Once more I barricaded myself inside, but I was better prepared this time. I rammed the door-wedge Mum used to prop open the back door and slammed a chair under the handle again. The door shook as it was shoved open by a centimetre but it jammed firmly. Although Uncle Calvin was pushing and shouting on the other side, the door held. Fearing he might kick it in, I bundled my laptop, front door key and a few other things into a bag which I strapped over my shoulder. Throwing my duvet out of the window, I scrambled out after it, jumped down to the flowerbed and ran to the shed.

Shut inside, with Merlin running to greet me, I sat hunched in the corner with my phone. I sent a text to Mum.

> Due to circumstances beyond my control,
> I can't Skype as planned. Sorry, but you'll get
> to see my lovely face tomorrow in HD. Hope
> all's good with you, Love Fin.

I stretched out my duvet, lay down with Merlin and began planning my next move. In the corner of the shed, beside the motor mower and under a rug, I had already hidden a packed suitcase. Although I'd expected an awkward start and was prepared for trouble, I didn't think our first day would be quite this bad.

I decided to sleep in the shed overnight and in the morning I would do something scary. I'd be going on a journey into the unknown – a trip that could well change everything. After all, anything was worth a try.

TWELVE

Sunlight streaming through cobwebs at the window and Merlin sitting on my neck woke me before six. I wondered where I was, as smells of grass cuttings, petrol and cat food were a bewildering cocktail to wake up to. But I was soon sitting out under the apple tree, watching Merlin explore the garden while I thought about the day ahead. I needed to weigh everything up, get things just right and keep my nerve – a bit like balancing stones, I thought.

Gingerly I climbed in through my bedroom window. At least my prison guards were unlikely to stir so early, as their boozing usually zonked them out until late. I could wash, dress and get some breakfast in the hope I wouldn't disturb them. Even so, it would be risky to stay for long indoors and face an ugly scene. So, with bag over my shoulder, I headed to Mrs Boughtwood's, hoping to do a deal with her. I sat on her front door step until she appeared at about 8 o'clock, in her dressing gown and clutching the watering can.

'My word, you're keen this morning, Finley. Let's hope for another good day of trade today, dear.'

'The thing is, Mrs Boughtwood, I'd like to do a deal with you. I've run into a bit of a problem. Do you mind if I don't do the shop today and ask a big favour? Is there any chance of a small loan from our takings – and can I leave my laptop and stuff here? I'll make up the time and pay back with interest – it's just that I need to buy a train ticket and go to Mum's hospital. It's a bit urgent, actually.'

She looked at me with a fixed smile for a long time. 'You must do as you think fit, Finley. How much to you need?'

'Fifty pounds should do it. I'm sorry to let you down, but I promise to get back on top of everything tomorrow.'

'The money isn't a problem, dear. Can I do anything to help?'

'Can you just tell Sophie I'll be back this evening to catch up and I'll tell her everything then.'

She nodded with a genuine smile this time. 'Of course. You've done Sophie the world of good, you know. She's a different girl this summer. Thank you.'

I didn't know what to say, other than, 'Great. Merlin is doing fine, by the way. He slept on me for most of the night. I could feel him purring against my neck. He's totally awesome.'

I left my bag in her back room, waved as she watered

her hanging baskets and then I headed to the railway station.

I was instantly out of my comfort zone, as I hadn't been on trains much. Although I'd got information online, in all the crowds I found it difficult to work out exactly where to go. It wasn't easy trying to ask the woman at the ticket office, because she was the other side of a glass screen and half the time I had no idea what she was saying. A queue built up behind me as I was taking so long. In the end she gave me a wad of tickets and a little timetable so I could work out where to change and how long it would take. So off I went to Platform 2, hoping I wouldn't get on the wrong train or get off at the wrong place.

The carriage was packed, but I found a seat by the window and spent the next half an hour staring out at the sunlit world flashing past. At times the track ran right next to the beach and it felt as if the zipping train was exactly that; a giant zip, unzipping land from sea. Whenever we slid through a tunnel in the cliffs I wondered if we'd unzip the solid rock above. Bursting out into sunlight again, the train left behind the solid world I knew, as it sped me towards the scary unknown.

I'd been counting off each station we stopped at and knew I had to change trains at the fifth. Most of the other passengers spilled out with me and I was swept along up steps and over a bridge to another platform. I squinted up at the departures screen, trying to work out where to go next, as the crowds dissolved around me and I was left by myself. I proudly figured out that my next train left in nine minutes from Platform 4. More steps, another footbridge, more squinting up at screens, but I made it to the right train, already there and waiting. Another hour and I'd arrive in hospital-land, or so I thought.

When the train at last pulled into a massive station, I had no idea where to go. For some reason, I'd assumed the hospital would be just there right by the track. People were charging around in all directions, all of them looking as if they knew exactly what they were doing and where they were going. I queued with them at a barrier and fed my ticket into a slot that snatched it from my fingers. It popped up again but the gates didn't open and however hard I pushed they wouldn't let me through. I didn't notice a guy in uniform shouting at me to go through another gate. He looked closely at my ticket, shrugged his shoulders and let me through. Of all the people in the crowd, why was it just my ticket that didn't work? Feeling like I must be jinxed and born unlucky, I headed out into the urban jungle outside the station. I stared around at the wide streets clogged with traffic and the towering buildings stretching in all directions. My heart sank – where next?

I asked a man in a suit, who I thought looked reasonably friendly, 'Excuse me – how do I get to the hospital?'

'Easy, son. Just lie in the road. The ambulance will do the rest!' He walked off laughing. I told myself to keep calm and try again.

'Can you tell me how to get to the hospital, please?' I asked a random woman in the crowd.

'Which one?' she said.

'Er … haematology?'

She shrugged, pulled a face and walked away with a look of disgust. Maybe she thought I'd said 'haemorrhoidology'. It took several attempts asking total strangers before a young student-looking guy pointed up a hill to a bus stop. 'Try there. Number twenty-one should do it.'

When a twenty-one bus eventually came, I went upstairs so I could keep a lookout for where to get off. With no sign of a hospital in sight, I thought I must have missed it so I asked a woman with a baby behind me.

'Couple more stops, love. I'm going myself. Follow us.'

When we got off the bus I stared in disbelief. 'Is this like another town?' I asked.

The woman laughed. 'Ain't you been here before, love? It's all the hospital. You can easy get lost, mind.'

I followed all the signs to reception where I asked a smiley woman in round red-framed glasses behind the desk. 'Where do I go for haematology?'

'You have to follow the blue signs. Zone D. Haematology and Oncology. Have you got an appointment letter?'

When I told her my mother was in for treatment her smile melted. 'Well it's not visiting hours, my dear. You'd better come back later.'

'I need to speak to one of the doctors,' I answered. 'It's quite urgent, actually.'

'You can't without an appointment, love. You'll have to talk to one of the staff in H and O. Follow the signs.' She turned back to her screen and I headed off down a maze of corridors, following the blue arrows until I entered doors below a sign saying Haematology Centre.

Another counter, another smiley woman in uniform. 'Hello, love – how can I help?'

'My mum is a patient here. Alison Rackman.'

'It's not visiting time yet, that's assuming she's allowed visitors … ' she tapped at a keyboard. 'Visiting has been restricted due to norovirus risks. Rackman, you say? It doesn't look as if she's here.'

'Well, I'm sure she is – but the thing is, I need to speak to one of her doctors. She needs a donor and I want to be tested to see if I can save her.'

She stopped typing and looked up at me with one of those pathetic looks I often seem to get. 'It's probably best if you talk to your GP, dear. We can't discuss these matters with you here … ah, yes, she's here on our system after all – in a single ward, restricted access. I suggest you come back in a couple of weeks and see if someone can help you then.'

'I've come a long way. It hasn't been easy. I need to see someone before then. I need to give a saliva sample.' I was trying my best to keep calm.

'You'll need an appointment for that.'

'Then please make one for me.'

'You'll need to speak to the specialist first.'

'That's what I'm trying to do!' By now I was shouting.

'If someone doesn't help me soon, I might end up shooting myself – or do I need an appointment to do that?'

The woman's eyes narrowed as she became more agitated. 'We have to follow certain procedures.'

'Yes, but my mum could be dying and I might be the only one who can save her. All I want is to talk to someone who can help us. I've come a long way by myself after sleeping in a shed all night. Why doesn't anyone care?'

She didn't look at me directly but pointed across the room. 'Take a seat. Someone will see to you when convenient.'

About half an hour later a woman in a white coat came and sat beside me. She looked through papers in her hand. 'You must be Finley,' she smiled.

I nodded. She kept smiling. 'Does Mum know you're here?'

I told her she didn't and I knew they probably wouldn't let me see her, but I'd come to see if I was a match for stem cells.

'Let's go to my room for a chat,' she said. She led me along a corridor to a small office with screens at one end pulled in front of a trolley bed. 'Take a seat, Finley. Tell me, has your mother explained her condition to you?'

'Yes, sort of. I've read about it. I know it's serious if she can't get a donor.'

She nodded and paused. 'Yes. She's being very brave and has been poorly for longer than you may realise. I'm sure she'd like to see you in a moment. You'll have to wear gowns and a mask as well as have a bit of a scrub.

It's very important she doesn't catch an infection at this stage.'

'I know. She's neutropenic. That means her white blood cells called neutrophils aren't working properly at fighting infections and stuff.'

'I'm very impressed with your knowledge, Finley.'

I told her I wanted to be a vet so I'd researched it online. 'Cats can have the same problem, you know. All mammals, I should think. I'm not sure about reptiles as they're cold-blooded.'

After smiling again, she became more serious. 'Finley, we don't know how long it will take for your mother to respond to treatment or whether we'll ever find a match for a stem cell transplant.'

'That's why I'm here,' I said. 'Can you do a test? I don't mind giving a blood sample or saliva. It's up to you.'

'I'm afraid we can't do that, Finley. I appreciate how you want to help but you must be at least sixteen to be considered. How old are you?'

'Fourteen in two days. I don't see that my cells aren't as good as a sixteen year old's. Mine might even be healthier. I don't smoke or drink or do drugs.'

'We can't accept cells from children. We'd get into trouble as it's all about medical ethics. The chances are you wouldn't be a match anyway. Maybe try in a couple of years, eh?'

I looked straight at her. 'I'm not stupid. I know as well as you that Mum won't last even a year if she doesn't get a cell transplant. How do you think I'll feel if she dies and then we find I could have saved her? How will that go down with your medical ethics?'

She looked awkward and shuffled about. 'Finley, I can tell you're a thoughtful boy and you mean well. I'll tell you what I'll do. I'll take a little swab of your saliva from inside your cheek just for the record. There's a high chance you won't be a match, but if it will put your mind at rest and show that you've tried, then all well and good.'

'I don't want to show anything. I want to save my mum and I don't care what it takes – even if you have to drill out my bone marrow from my spine with a Black and Decker hammer drill without anaesthetic.'

She actually laughed this time. 'I can see you're a determined young man. Come on, let's find the equipment for your saliva sample. Then I'll take you to see your mother – how's that?'

After I'd had a couple of mouth swabs, my skin was wiped with antibacterial gel before I had to put on gloves, a white gown, cap and facemask. I looked like one of those CSI guys on TV shows. My first words to Mum when I entered her room were, 'Ah, this looks like the crime scene,' but she didn't hear because of my facemask and she was lying on the bed wearing headphones. She didn't recognise me either – until a nurse tapped her on the shoulder, removed the headphones and whispered in her ear. She sat up and looked at me for a long time, her face pale and yellowish.

'Fin?'

The nurse gave her a facemask to put on but she pushed it away.

'That's the last thing we need. He must see my face, however sad it looks.'

'I'm afraid you can't touch each other,' the nurse instructed. 'No physical contact. Sorry.'

Mum beckoned me, still trying to glimpse my face. 'Come closer, Fin. Let me see you. What are you doing here? Did Uncle Calvin bring you? Bless him.'

'I came on the train.'

She looked horrified. 'On your own?'

'Impressed?'

'Oh Fin, darling … but you shouldn't. I'm proud of you, of course, but you know how I worry. I can't believe you did all that by yourself, love.'

'Because you're worth it!' I said in my cheesiest voice, which probably didn't have much effect through the facemask.

'I've never been more desperate to give you a hug. Come closer … '

'You'd better not, Mum, or the hospital police will rush in and prise us apart and I'll be thrown in the hospital dungeon with all the bedpans.'

She smiled and looked up at the bottle of liquid feeding into her through a tube.

'What do you think of all this paraphernalia? Look, I put your lovely card in pride of place on the locker. It made me blub when I read it. Did you see my blog?'

'Of course. Sorry I didn't Skype. I told you I'd appear in HD – here I am in 3D. Little did you know you'd see me in the flesh.'

'How's Calvin?'

'Fine. They send their love. More to the point, how are you?' I wasn't sure if she believed my lie or whether she was just prepared to go along with it.

'Not too bad at the moment. Horrible taste in my mouth. You'll have to read my next blog for all the gory details. I'll do a bumper blog for your birthday. Have you had any birthday cards yet?'

I told her I hadn't, and was surprised when she answered, 'Good.'

When she saw my frown above the mask she just said, 'I asked Uncle Calvin to collect any early cards and give them to you on Thursday. I want you to have a lovely day and I'm afraid it'll be your first birthday ever that I'm not able to share with you. I'm so sorry.'

'We can still share it at a distance,' I said, but we both knew that wouldn't be the same. I so wanted to tell her about Uncle Calvin, how I'd had to sleep in the shed and how I was getting frightened of him. I wanted to ask her about the paper she had signed, making him my legal guardian, but I decided it was best to say nothing in case she got upset. I just wanted her to feel better and be cheerful.

'I've just given a saliva sample,' I said. 'When I read your blog and how donors are needed, I wanted to come and offer my stem cells. There's a chance I might be a match for you, seeing as I've got your amazing genes. Wouldn't that be fantastic?'

'Bless you, love. If only you were a few years older.

I've already asked them if your cells would work for me. Even if they put you on the register, you'll have to be at least sixteen to be a donor. I might not last that long.'

I tried to cheer her up by telling her about Mrs Boughtwood's shop and what we'd raised so far for Guide Dogs. She seemed to show interest and then insisted on a nurse taking a photo of us staging an exaggerated hug without touching, with her facemask back on. 'That will go on my blog to show the world what a wonderful son I have.'

I feared that would take some explaining to Uncle Calvin if he saw it, but right then I didn't care. I just wanted her to feel happier – like she used to be. I could tell she was getting tired and struggling to keep talking, so I said I'd better be heading back. She insisted that the nurse wrapped up the sandwiches she couldn't eat when I left 'to make sure you don't waste away', and then we said our goodbyes. Not being able to hold each other and the thought of returning home alone suddenly filled me with a kind of heavy dread inside. I was glad I was able to hide behind the facemask, but as I turned at the door for a final wave I felt a churning inside. Seeing Mum lying there so helpless and lonely, being filled by tubes with toxic chemicals, my head filled with screams again. I walked away sobbing – just making it into the corridor before I fell to my knees in tears and was violently sick over the polished terracotta tiles.

'You look like a zombie with a hangover,' Sophie told me, as we packed away the shop at the front gate.

'Yeah – I feel like one after that journey. I got lost when I left the hospital – don't ask why. I was too busy thinking about Mum and getting angry that they won't let me donate my stem cells. Why do grown-ups just ignore me all the time? It's the same with the hand on the beach. I've done my best to get adults to listen but they don't want to know. Should I give up or do something crazy to make them listen?'

'It's even worse when you're sitting in a wheelchair. Everyone ignores you. Hey, does your uncle drive a red car by any chance?'

I nodded and dreaded what was coming next. 'Well I think it was him who drove past here earlier. The woman in the passenger seat got out and came over to look at our stuff. She was a bit on the large side, dressed in big black baggy skirt and top, Goth-style jewellery, ultra thick black makeup, dark lipstick and Gothy hair with red highlights.'

'Yeah, that's Jasmine,' I said. 'What did she want?'

'She looked at your cards and asked where Fin was, so I just said you'd gone away for the day. She looked through the books to see if there was any steampunk, then snorted and waddled back to the car. Then they drove off. Weird.'

I told her how I tried to keep out of their way, but I didn't admit I'd slept in the shed to avoid them.

As we were packing away the last of my cards, Lian arrived – still a bundle of energy and talking so fast I wasn't sure what all the excitement was about.

'I've just done my first shift at The Actor's Creak. I've made loads of mistakes, but I'm learning fast and tomorrow I should have chance to chat to the others about Ella. Tonight's my first night in her caravan, so maybe soon you can come and join me there for a meal and we'll look for clues. I'll cook you some proper Chinese food – in a wok on a wobbly old gas ring.'

She then spoke more slowly and seriously. 'I phoned the police just now. They still haven't identified the body they found on the beach. I asked if they'd like me to go and check if it's my missing friend, and they want me to go as soon as possible. I'm really not looking forward to it. I asked if they knew the cause of death yet and they said there were no suspicious circumstances. Apparently there were head injuries and a broken neck "consistent with a fall from a height". They said they get several suicides off the cliffs every year, so they asked me if my friend might have taken her own life. I told them, "NO WAY!" That's one thing Ella would never do. But they just said, "You'd be surprised. Never say never." I'm sure if Ella was in such a bad way she'd have phoned me. I'm also sure she's fine and having a great time somewhere. I'll soon find out where she's gone.'

Sophie's gran insisted we all stayed for a meal, so by the time I got home it was late. Although there was no car parked outside, for the first time ever I dreaded walking in my own front door. A heavy weight seemed to sink from my throat into the pit of my stomach as I slipped my key in the lock. Without Mum around and with Uncle Calvin's presence lingering like a vile smell, I couldn't force myself to go inside. It was a golden opportunity to creep in and search for the signed paper stating they were now in charge of me, but right then I didn't have the energy or courage. Finding and destroying that document could wait till the morning.

I slipped my key from the lock and walked down the side path to the shed. At least Merlin gave me a warm welcome and was all over me, mainly because he'd finished all his food. So, after I'd fed him and told him what I was planning for tomorrow, we both lay on my duvet in the warm stillness, among familiar and strangely comforting smells. Sleeping here for a second night was far preferable to being indoors with all its demons.

As I dozed in the sticky heat, I was unaware of the storm brewing over the sea and slowly creeping inland. My dream was of Grandad again – and far from the thunder clouds rolling in over the cliffs and about to engulf the night.

THIRTEEN

Bursts of lightning flashed through the shiny wet window as the shed floor trembled. Merlin snuggled into me nervously, but I only stirred briefly. Even drips falling on my neck didn't wake me for long and I slept soundly till long after it was light. By then the storm had passed and misty rays of sunlight broke through the rising steam on the lawn. Merlin stepped on the damp grass gingerly, then shook his paws and darted back in the shed. I fed him a tin of cat food, left him extra plates of milk and kitten munchies, then went indoors to get washed and dressed, hoping no one would be awake.

Very slowly I slid my door key in the lock and pushed open the front door, trying not to make a sound. There was a letter to Mum on the doormat and a birthday card for me in a blue envelope – a day early. I took the card to open later and I crept along the hall to my bedroom door, where I stared in disbelief. The door had gone, with just a bare doorframe and marks where the hinges had been removed. Inside my room, it looked as if burglars had struck, with cupboards and drawers open and all my stuff thrown around the room. Even my mattress was hanging off the bed, which had been dragged across the floor.

Rage shot through me like a thousand volts and I bit my clenched fist, trying to keep control – tasting blood and wincing at the pain. Knowing the bedroom raider was my own uncle, I was gobsmacked that even he could do this. I so wanted to barge in his room and throw everything at him, but I was determined not to let him grind me down and break me.

I walked into my room, took a deep breath and sat on the bed with my head in my hands, telling myself again and again to remain calm and ride the storm.

Still taking great care not to make a sound, I packed a few things in a bag, including my birthday card. Then I washed and changed in the kitchen, rather than in the bathroom, right next to where my obnoxious uncle was probably snoring smugly and dreaming up more ways to make my life a misery.

After gulping down a bowl of cornflakes, I was ready to get on my way, so I tiptoed to the front door. Just as I reached out to open it, a hand grabbed my shoulder and spun me round. I was face to face with the smouldering scowl of Uncle Calvin, whose eyes looked wild, like a wolf's about to attack its prey.

'Unlucky. The water pipes make a noise. They woke me,' he snarled.

'Morning, Uncle Calvin.' I tried to appear unflustered but he clearly wasn't interested in small talk.

'Get in that kitchen now,' he snapped, before calling over his shoulder to Jasmine. I dreaded to think what she would be wearing if she'd just got up, so I didn't dare look at the enormous shadow appearing at their door. He gripped my chin between his finger and thumb to make me look at him as he spoke. 'We are going to have a talk and it's time you understand we mean business. Where the hell have you been?'

I surprised myself at how calm I managed to stay, despite my head feeling like it might erupt, as the anger and hatred welled up again. But I wasn't going to let him see he could upset me. I knew he wanted to make me scared and I wasn't going to give him the pleasure of letting him get the better of me.

'Nowhere,' I said. 'I've just got up – like you.'

He was dressed in a tee shirt and boxers, with stubble over his bloated chin.

'You can't hide from us anymore,' he sneered dangerously. 'You can no longer shelter behind closed doors and it's no use trying to lock yourself in the bathroom, either. I've removed the lock. You can't escape.'

I was speechless. I could smell drink on his breath but his eyes flashed with something more sinister. 'Are you crazy?' I muttered.

His hand tightened on my neck and pulled me

towards him. 'You've got a choice. You can either come to the kitchen calmly and do as you're told – or we can do it the other way, where you'll get hurt. It's up to you.'

'Are you threatening me, Uncle Calvin?'

'I'm telling you.'

'But why have you messed up my room? That's totally out of order.'

'You're about to find out.' He pulled me into the kitchen, where he dragged a chair into the middle of the floor. Jasmine, in a weird leopard-print dressing gown far too small for her, came and stood beside it like a prison guard, gripping a leather belt.

'Are you going to hit me with that?' I asked.

'That's up to you,' she warned. 'If you need restraining, I will respond.'

'Where did you spend the night?' Uncle Calvin asked menacingly, leaning over me – scarily close.

'Here,' I answered, knowing full-well that would annoy him.

'The truth!' Jasmine spat, whipping the belt across my legs and making me squeal, more from shock than pain.

'The thunder kept us up half the night, so we were in and out of your room,' he said slowly. 'You were NOT here at all and you've got some explaining to do. Where were you yesterday? We went looking for you. You're my responsibility and I take such matters seriously.'

'If you must know,' I began, 'I went to see Mum in hospital. If you don't believe me, look at a picture of us on her blog.'

I knew that would make him react. His eyes glared and his lip quivered.

'What did you tell her?' He looked furious, while Jasmine paced up and down muttering, with a face like thunder. With her hair all over the place and without her make-up on, she looked even scarier than usual, with puffy eyes and a gross saggy mouth. I did my best to look up with sad puppy eyes.

'I told her I loved her, if you must know. I also went to offer my stem cells, seeing as you refused yours.'

Inside my head, I shouted, 'Yes!' when I saw how they were both lost for words. They glanced at each other, not knowing what to say next.

'Who took you?' Jasmine asked, clearly irritated.

'I went by myself on the train.'

'I don't believe you,' she frowned. 'Where did you get the money?'

'I borrowed some – seeing as Uncle Calvin stole mine.'

He grabbed my collar. 'No I didn't. What did you say to her about us?'

'Mum asked about you, so I said you were fine and sent your love. Was I wrong?'

They looked at each other awkwardly and moved away into the hall, where they presumably discussed tactics now that I'd out-witted them by seeing Mum without them knowing.

I stayed in the chair until Uncle Calvin returned, looking serious and agitated but slightly less threatening.

'Right,' he barked, 'Pay attention. Like I've said, you

do as I say from now on. I've got three rules. If you obey to our satisfaction, I will relax the first two and you can continue to come and go as you please. No interference from us provided you agree. If not, we turn nasty and we'll make your life hell. Got it?'

I nodded, even though I didn't really understand what he was actually telling me. He grabbed another chair, put it directly in front of me with its back towards me, then he sat astride it, folding his arms across the top and resting his chubby chin on them. 'Rule number one: no more coming and going as you like. You must ask my permission and discuss your plans for each day. Rule number two: no more use of laptop or phone without my consent and approval. I've already disconnected the wi-fi. Rule three: you hand over Grandad's biscuit tin immediately.'

It took all my self control not to swear and call him all the names I could think of – but I knew that's what he wanted. Instead, I tried to out-smart him.

'Ah, so that's why you've turned my room upside down. You thought I had biscuits belonging to Grandad.' In fact, it hadn't crossed my mind it was the tin in the wardrobe they wanted. Obviously they hadn't lifted the false bottom and found it, and I imagined Grandad smiling at me, saying, 'Well done – you've kept his grubby paws off our secret tin.'

I felt myself smile back, as I replied, 'I'm afraid I can't really help you, Uncle Calvin. There are some biscuits in the cupboard over there if you're hungry.'

He sprang to his feet and leaned over me. 'Shut up.

You know full well this isn't about biscuits. I know what's in that tin, you know. It's my inheritance. My grandfather's medals are in that tin. So are my grandmother's and my mum's gold rings and jewellery. They now belong to me and I intend to get them back. They could fetch a fortune and I want them now.'

'They could still be in Grandad's flat somewhere,' I said, knowing that he would already have searched high and low.

'You know very well where that tin is. You had my father round your little finger, you scheming little parasite. You got him to change his will, didn't you? Well, I'm going to make sure I get my full whack. I want your signature on a document I've had drawn up to say you give up your share of the proceeds of his estate when his flat gets sold in the next few weeks.'

So now I knew his game. I didn't even know about Grandad's will, but I wasn't surprised he hadn't left Uncle Calvin much.

'What if I don't agree?' I asked.

He bristled and gave a twisted grin. 'You will regret it. Soon you will beg me to allow you to sign. Besides, you're forgetting something. I have a signed document to say I am now your legal guardian while your mum is off the scene. That means when the money is released soon, your share will come directly to me to manage for you, as you're only a minor. So you see, I'll get my hands on it anyway. In the meantime, I want that biscuit tin. Where is it?'

'I wish I could help you, Uncle Calvin. I'd like to see it myself, as what's inside it sounds really interesting.'

Jasmine took one step forward and slapped me round the face. It didn't just sting like mad, it really shocked me as I didn't see it coming. I felt my eyes watering as my cheek burned. While I sat stunned and speechless, Uncle Calvin fixed me a long stare. Somehow I managed to stare back without looking away or blinking. That really annoyed him, as he knew I was lying, but I was staying cool and defiant. He looked furious – not just with me but with Jasmine. He shouted at her and told her to get out of the room, before turning back to me with his nose almost touching mine.

'I'll give you till tomorrow to think very carefully, as I hold the trump card. If I so choose, I can have you taken into care and you'll be sent away. I just have to report you to the authorities as being unmanageable and the courts will take over. That would kill your mother, of course – so you'd better think long and hard. You'd be unwise to mention this conversation to her, as well. I will not be held responsible if you cause your own mother to lose her will to live.'

That did it. My anger exploded and I spat in his face.

'Blackmail and bullying won't work on me!' I jumped up, ran past him, pushed Jasmine out of my way, shouted all the obscenities I knew, grabbed my bag, wrenched open the front door and threw myself outside. I had no idea what they were yelling at me as I kicked his car and ran off down the road.

I was still seething when I lay panting and choking on Mrs Boughtwood's doorstep. With tears streaming and my nose running like a tap, I sat there alone until Sophie arrived. I knew I looked a mess, but I didn't care – I hadn't let that vile man delight in seeing me cry.

'What's up?' Sophie asked, as she waved to her mum driving off.

'Stuff at home. My uncle's in a strop. Another row. Do you think your gran might let me stay here tonight while things cool off? Maybe tomorrow she'll let me get Merlin and perhaps we could stay in the spare bedroom. Would she let me, do you reckon – seeing as it's my birthday tomorrow?'

'I don't see why not. I expect she'd be delighted. Let's go and ask her.'

Mrs Boughtwood was mopping out the garage. 'This place always floods after a storm,' she shrugged. 'At least it gives the floor a good wash.'

When Sophie asked if I could stay a few nights in the spare bedroom, she beamed. 'It will be my pleasure, dear. Any excuse to bake a birthday cake, as well. I'd like to see Merlin again, so bring him over when you like. The shop is making lots of money, so you're already earning your keep, Finley.'

Our shop did well during the day and nearly all my packs of cards had sold by the time Lian arrived. As soon as she appeared, we knew the worst. Her usual energy and enthusiasm had disappeared and I could tell immediately that something was wrong. After we went indoors, Lian sat on the sofa and dabbed at her eyes with a tissue.

'It was her,' she said at last. 'I've been to identify the body. It was definitely Ella. I still can't believe it. The little butterfly tattoo on her shoulder, the earring I gave her – the other was missing, her lovely face – it was her all right. Poor Ella didn't deserve this. I just hope she didn't suffer.'

'Did you tell the police about her sandal and bag on the beach – and how she'd been buried, then disappeared?' I asked.

'They are convinced Ella fell or jumped over the cliff in the dark, got covered in sand and shingle by the high tide and was then dragged out to sea by the next tide, which was probably higher and stronger as it was a full moon shortly after she disappeared. The police think there's nothing suspicious and there's no reliable evidence to make this a murder enquiry. I told them everything you told me, Fin, but they didn't seem to think you were a reliable witness. Sorry.'

Sophie was more annoyed than me. 'That's ridiculous. Aren't they going to investigate *anything*?'

'They'll now confirm it's Ella by checking her dental records, then notify her parents and search her flat, but they said if there are no grounds to suggest "involvement by a third party", as they put it, the case will be closed and her body will be released for burial. They accused me of being over-dramatic and of watching too many murder dramas on TV. Dozens of people die along this coast each year from natural causes, and apparently more people were killed in drowning or falls along the British coast last year than everyone who died in cycling accidents in the whole country.'

'So that's it, then,' I said. 'End of.'

'Not quite,' Lian added with a touch of mystery. 'I found out something at work that I need to follow up. I owe it to Ella to find out more. Can you both come for supper to my caravan tomorrow night to talk more – and to light candles in memory of her? Hey, it will be for your birthday, too. We'll make it special.'

It was great to be in a real bed again and without the need to barricade the door.

I lay and thought about Ella and how, although I'd never met her, I owed it to her to find the truth about what had happened in her last hours. I was looking forward to the morning to see what else we could do – and I would Skype Mum for my birthday. I sent her an email and read hers, as well as her latest blog.

> They take my blood pressure every few hours – day and night. Sleep isn't easy!
>
> I am not sure how many units of blood I'll get through by the end of this treatment, but I've already had dozens of transfusions since I was first diagnosed. A unit of blood usually makes me feel much better with more energy, taking away some of the tiredness. My platelets need topping up every couple of days.

I have to keep to a 'clean diet'. Chemotherapy damages the gut lining, making it easier for bacteria to cross into the bloodstream. I need to avoid most fresh food, so it's unhealthy eating that's allowed – like crisps, tinned puddings, muffins and fizzy drinks. What fun!

They tell me it could be at least a week after this chemo finishes when I'll start seeing/feeling the effects. Fingers crossed.

More soon, Ali.

I lay for a long time thinking about Mum and all that had happened since our crazy walk by the waves, just a few evenings before. I knew she'd left me a present and card at home, but I didn't fancy going back to get them. It was then I remembered the card I'd put in my bag earlier, so I took it out to see who it was from. I didn't recognise the handwriting on the dark blue envelope – with a stamp and postmark from the USA. Not knowing anyone in America, I tore open the envelope eagerly and looked at the card showing a kid on a skateboard with a big 14 in shiny gold numbers. But it was what was inside that made me stare like a zombie for the next hour, completely dumbfounded. In fact, I couldn't sleep for hours. It wasn't because of the £50 in ten-pound notes that slid out onto the floor, but from just five words written inside in neat, italic handwriting.

To Finley – love from Dad.

FOURTEEN

Thursday 25th August

My fourteenth birthday. Goodbye unlucky thirteen. *As if.*

The mystery birthday card was such a bolt from the blue that it disturbed me. With everything else going on, I was getting mega stressy. So I got up early and crept out to clean the animal pens in the garage. I told all the cats the only way I could deal with a message from a dad I knew nothing about was to blot it (and him) from my mind – not that I even knew what he looked like. No photos of him existed. At least the fifty pounds would come in handy.

As I went online to talk to Mum, I wondered if I should mention the card. She always refused to talk about my dad and, as her face appeared on my screen, I knew this wasn't the best time to ask. She looked worse than I'd ever seen her. 'Happy birthday, love,' she said feebly. 'Sorry

I look so rough. I've got a lung infection and feel terrible. Has Uncle Calvin given you your cards yet?'

'Just one card so far.' I was about to say it was from America to see what she'd say, when the picture on my screen froze and we lost contact. My heart sank as I realised how ill she was. I'd call her back later.

There wasn't time to get upset, as Sophie arrived with balloons and party poppers. Breakfast turned out to be a marathon, with cake, trifle, ice cream, bananas and lashings of maple syrup. By the time I'd opened their cards and presents, it was midday – when I borrowed a cat basket and went back home to collect Merlin.

My uncle's car was nowhere to be seen, so it was a great relief to enter the front door without having to tiptoe everywhere and risk bumping into anyone. The familiar hallway and my doorless bedroom no longer felt like home. There were different smells – Jasmine's cigarette smoke had already seeped into the walls. Ugliness hung in the air and seemed to be spreading like a disease through every room. I felt I didn't belong here anymore.

I stood for a long time at the door to Uncle Calvin's room. Somewhere inside was the piece of paper my mum had signed, making him my legal guardian. So was my money he'd taken. It was time to play him at his own game and search his room. After a quick glance over my shoulder, I pushed the door open and stepped inside. The room was a mess, with beer cans and bottles on the floor, clothes all over the place and the smell of stale smoke – probably cannabis. I carefully opened drawers but there wasn't much inside, other than a pile of Jasmine's large knickers. I dreaded touching them, but I slid my hand underneath and felt an envelope – the very envelope with my two hundred pounds inside. I quickly stuffed it in my pocket and carried on rummaging through a wardrobe. I wondered if this one had a false bottom like the one in my room, so I stooped down to check. Just as I tried to squeeze my fingers into a gap, a hand grabbed my sleeve and wrenched me out onto the floor. I fell back and stared up at Uncle Calvin, who was staring down, grinning creepily. 'Looking for Narnia, I suppose.'

'Yeah,' I managed to croak. 'Mister Tumnus sends his love.'

He reached down and held out his hand. 'Up you get. Happy birthday.'

He must have seen the shock in my face. I was expecting a thumping, or worse. His sudden change of tactic into a chummy uncle was somehow more frightening than his usual nastiness. At least I knew where I was when he was being normal, but now he was pretending to be friendly, I was terrified.

As I got to my feet, he patted me on the back. 'Fancy a coffee? Jasmine's putting the kettle on. Your mum's left you a fancy birthday cake – take a look.'

I couldn't believe what was happening and when I saw the awesome cake with fourteen marzipan stones balanced on the top, I felt a tear drip down my cheek. It was almost like the embarrassing scene in the garden centre all over again – but somehow I felt even worse. This time I was so desperate to hug Mum, the pain of our separation was choking me – as I looked at her brilliant handiwork, but without her being there to share it.

'Sorry about this,' I spluttered. 'It must be the hormones. When you hit fourteen all hell lets loose.' I tried to smile but I was met by stony faces.

'I've put your birthday cards on the table,' Jasmine said coldly. 'There aren't many, seeing as you don't have friends.'

I ignored her, as I didn't want to take my eyes off Mum's cake. In that moment I missed her more than any time I'd known, and all I wanted was to be alone and admire her masterpiece. Without looking at Jasmine, I managed to mutter, 'I prefer quality to quantity,' with a shrug to say, *So what?* then added, 'Anyway, I've already had cards from my close friends. I've put them with the card from America.'

Uncle Calvin swore. 'Him? With money in it, I suppose. Damn, you weren't meant to see it. I promised her.'

As if I wasn't surprised and confused already, I stared at him before I finally asked, 'Did you know him – my dad?'

'Don't go there. Of course I knew him – better than anyone else. I always told her he was different. Too different. Too clever, too. I'll never forgive him for what he did. Your mum told me to make sure you didn't see that card. He sends one every year, but she always burns them and keeps the money till you're eighteen. You'd best not tell her.'

I didn't understand. 'Why doesn't she talk about him? I've tried asking her.'

'After what happened? I reckon their bust-up caused your problem – or you caused his. You'll probably go the same way.'

'What way? What do you mean?'

'What sort of guy leaves his wife and kid to run off with another bloke? It's sick, that's what it is. He married him, too. No wonder you're not right. No wonder she's never been the same. No wonder she burnt her wedding photos. If he shows up at the funeral, I'll personally smash his face in.'

'Funeral?'

'The hospital just phoned. Your mum's now got pneumonia. She won't last long now. Get real, lad – in her condition it's the kindest and quickest way to go. Then you'll be handed over to me officially for the next four years – what's known as legal custody. I'll soon lick you into shape, so get used to it, sunshine.'

I stared at him in disbelief. I'd thought I was used to his change in moods and his weird streak, but he was becoming scarier every time he spoke. He soon slipped back to his old self when he spoke to Jasmine.

'I caught him in our room, Jas. Thieving little git was in the wardrobe. I know what he was looking for – the document declaring I now have custody of him. Unlucky, lad – it's safely locked in the car where your thieving little paws won't find it.'

'Talking of paws, are you going to tell him?' Jasmine sneered.

His hand shot up as if he was stopping the traffic. 'Wait, love.'

Turning to me, his eyes narrowed and glared with spite. 'I've tried to be nice to you, Finley. You know I can be reasonable. But if you don't hand over that biscuit tin, you're in for a rough ride. Birthday or not, you're grounded from now on, till you tell me where it is and where you've been staying. And don't think you can go charging off on that bike of yours anymore. I've declared it unsafe and tied it up so you can't use it. It's out of bounds. So is the shed.'

My blood froze. He'd been out there. I ran past him, through the back door and down the garden to where the shed door was swinging open in the breeze. As I stepped inside, I saw my bike tied up with masses of rope. My duvet and blanket had gone and so had Merlin's dishes. But where was Merlin?

I turned to shout at Uncle Calvin behind me on the path. 'Where is he?'

'I've given the place a clear-out,' he snapped. 'I thought my dad's tin might be in there. Your fault. You should have told me where it is.'

'Where is he? Where's Merlin?' I was screaming as I ran at him.

He grabbed my wrist. 'Some idiot left food in there. There were flies and rats so I had to do something.' He was smiling – an evil, sickening smirk. 'I saw something dark and furry run out through that flap. Rats need dealing with, so that's what I did. We can't have vermin out here, can we?'

I spat in his face and ran back to the shed, where I froze in horror. There were small heaps of blue poison pellets in each corner. 'Where's my kitten? What have you done to him?'

He was still smiling smugly. 'We don't do cats. Jasmine's got an allergy. We have to get rid of them on grounds of health and safety.'

He gave a weird chuckle and a shrug before turning to walk back indoors, looking very pleased with himself. Jasmine was watching from the kitchen window, laughing hysterically as I ran around frantically trying to find Merlin. I kept calling his name as I crawled round the back of the shed, peered over fences into neighbours' gardens and scrambled under all the shrubs. My head was spinning as I searched and searched, calling, shouting, desperate to find him. As well as the anger and hatred screaming inside my head, I was furious with myself for leaving Merlin on his own. I should have known better, and the rage for my own stupidity now fed on my rage for those evil monsters laughing at me indoors. Rage at Mum's illness and at a dad who'd abandoned us poured more fuel on the flames now burning me up inside. Rage on rage on rage.

When I saw Merlin's lifeless body behind the compost heap, the rage burst out – an explosion of anger I'd never known before. My insides heaved and I threw up my giant breakfast over the lawn. A soupy banana spew stuck in my nose and throat as I sobbed helplessly and held Merlin's cold, stiff body, desperately trying to revive him. I knew it was hopeless and at last, hugging him tightly in my arms,

I went back to the shed for a spade. Hardly able to see through my streaming eyes and screwed-up face, I buried him by the apple tree, as I dribbled, spluttered and struggled for breath. I tasted my salty tears and the banana snot running from my nose. I no longer cared if Merlin's killers saw me in such a state. They'd gone too far this time. They'd broken me and they knew it, as they laughed triumphantly at the kitchen window.

They had won the battle, but I was determined they hadn't won the war. It was up to me to show them I could fight back.

Apart from churning fury wrenching my stomach, my brain was shouting just two things: revenge and escape. I had to make them sorry and get away from them for good. In that instant, something exploded inside me and I went ballistic. Storming into the kitchen, I swore at full blast, shouting all the insults I could think of. The 'explosive disorder' gene was letting rip and I was terrified.

'It's only a cat, for God's sake,' Jasmine shrugged. 'Get over it and man up.'

They sat grinning – but what riled me was seeing them drinking, smoking and eating my birthday cake. 'What's yours is ours now,' Jasmine scoffed, as she cut another slice.

The next thing happened so fast. I snatched the knife, tipped over the table and ran outside, with her and the cake sprawling over the floor. I didn't look back but ran to the shed to cut my bike free with the kitchen knife. I soon sliced through all the knots and was pulling the bike away when I kicked a petrol can by the lawn mower. It was all I needed.

Seething with uncontrollable rage, I grabbed the can and a box of bonfire matches, then sped on my bike through the side gate, out onto the road. Stopping at the front of Uncle Calvin's car, I slammed the petrol can at the windscreen. Cracks snaked across and splintered, but the glass held. After two more thumps with the corner of the can, the glass shattered. I punched a hole through and in seconds I was pouring petrol over the dashboard and front seats. I threw the can onto the back seat, struck a match and threw it in.

Jumping on my bike, I sped off down the road, only glancing back when I got to the end – as flames ripped through the whole car, pouring black smoke through the smashed windscreen. I punched the air with a yelp – I was free, and that signed paper was about to go up in smoke. Revenge. Escape. Mission accomplished.

I didn't stop pedalling till I reached the top of the cliff road. Gasping for breath and with my heart about to burst, I flopped onto a grassy bank near the caravan park. I lay on my back, staring up at the clear blue sky … with a column of smoke belching high above the town and drifting inland in a rolling dark cloud.

It was only then I thought about what I'd done and what trouble I'd be in. But I couldn't get the sight of Merlin's body from my mind – and that monster who'd deliberately poisoned him to make me obey them. Now I understood Grandad's warning never to trust that man –

who I realised was far worse than I'd ever imagined. He was some kind of disturbed control-freak who'd stop at nothing to grind me down. I loathed him and never wanted to see either of them again.

I rode on in a daze till I reached the top of the cliff, then left my bike under the same bush as before and zigzagged my way down the path to the beach. It was almost high tide and no one was around. I was surprised to see one of my stone towers still standing just as I'd left it, so I sat beside it. No way would I be able to build something like that again – not without inner calm to keep a steady hand. My life was now a mess and falling apart, so I stroked one of the stones in the hope of connecting with my old self. In an instant they all toppled and fell at my feet. I sat in the sand and stared at the rubble – thinking about the rubble of my own life and wondering if I'd ever be able to put things back together again.

A warm breeze blew in off the sea and I began to feel totally empty … numb … sleepy. Not having slept much the night before and after all the turmoil of the day, I was shattered. I lay down at the foot of the cliff, at the exact spot where I'd seen the hand, and I sent Mum a text.

> Hi Mum, Hope U R feeling better. Thanx so much for great cake. ☺ Also the brill pressie. Don't worry about me – staying with friends. Fell out with Uncle C. Sorry. If he comes to see you a) don't believe him b) don't sign anything. Will talk soon. Love u loads – Fin X

It was only then I realised I hadn't even opened

Mum's present she'd left for me on her bed. I felt bad about that, but there was no way I would go back for it – just one more regret to add to my growing list.

Surprisingly, with so much swirling around my head, I felt myself drifting off. I lay back on the sand, warmed by the sun, with waves sliding gently up the beach nearby – the tide beginning to turn … and I slipped into the deepest sleep. My darkest thoughts and fears drifted away … beyond reach … until I'd have to wake and face the world once more.

I was dragged from sleep by what I thought was a massive storm. Sand and spray blew over me and I opened my eyes to see a looming shadow hovering above, swirling and flashing. Flying grit stung my eyes as helicopter rotor blades whipped the beach into a whirlwind. My immediate instinct was to hide, so I rolled into the cliff beside me, under a jutting slab of rock. The helicopter hung a few metres above the waves breaking down the beach. Squinting out through the sandstorm, I saw the tide had gone out a fair way, so I must have slept a long time. I looked at my watch – ten to six.

The helicopter rose, banked towards the sea and circled the beach once more, then swept over the headland into the next bay. I had no idea if it was a police helicopter or the coastguards, but I couldn't help thinking they might be looking for a kid on the run. An arsonist, maybe.

Remaining very still under the hanging rock while my brain tried to wake up, I blinked up at the rust-red cliff. As my eyes began to focus, I was aware of a row of pebbles along the foot of the cliff – ideal for stone-balancing. But it was something glinting on one of the boulders that caught my eye. I reached out to pick it up – a silver USB memory stick with a sliding on-off switch on its side. Instinctively I stuffed it in my pocket, then crawled out into the evening sun. Still coming-to, I squinted at my phone and saw a couple of texts. One from Mum told me to get in touch and another from Sophie told me the police had called on her gran, looking for me, followed by a shouty man who she thought was my uncle. Her text finished with:

> Best keep away from here. Meet you at
> Lian's at 6.30pm. 52 Clifftop Caravan Park.
> Mum will bring me. Take care. P.S. I don't
> believe a word they say about you. ☺
> Soph X.

I sent replies, then walked down the beach to the sea where I paddled, washed my face and tried to get rid of the dried sick on my T-shirt. My clothes and hair soon dried in the warm breeze as I climbed up the cliff path, got on my bike and rode to the caravan park. Number fifty-two was a small caravan facing a much larger deluxe mobile home with a sign saying RECEPTION. I guessed it was where Bryn Griffiths lived as, close by, a small shed had a muzzled shaved dog tethered to it, beside a smouldering incinerator. Wisps of smoke rose lazily before being caught by the breeze, while all around the ground was blackened and crusted with ash. The dog, just like the pit bull terrier I'd seen at the vet's, had no water bowl and the poor thing sat panting, watching me as I knocked on the door of number fifty-two. Not many people were about, apart from an elderly couple sitting on deckchairs outside their caravan and a few children playing in a field where a cattle truck was parked.

The caravan door opened and Lian swept me inside, as if I shouldn't be seen. 'Come in, Fin. Are you all right? Sophie's here – she's told me about you and the police. We've just read the news. What a birthday you're having!'

'My gran says it must be someone else and not you,' Sophie said. 'You couldn't possibly do all that.' She showed me the local news page on her phone.

TEENAGER ON RAMPAGE

A fourteen year-old boy (who cannot be named for legal reasons) is described by police as 'out of control and missing' after violently attacking two adults with a knife in their kitchen, followed by an arson attack on their car which was totally destroyed in a fireball in a quiet residential area of the town. Police, fire engines and an ambulance rushed to the scene in Hillside Road around 2.00pm when a distressed woman raised the alarm, reporting she had been savagely attacked with a sharp knife. She is said to be 'comfortable' and recovering from shock at home.

Fire crews fought a major street-fire, as heat from the blazing car was so intense it cracked windows in nearby properties, as well as destroying a hedge and fence. Breathing gear had to be worn by fire-fighters, who later confirmed the vehicle had been totally destroyed, as well as a lamppost and a wheelie bin.

A man at the scene told reporters the youth responsible was his nephew who, despite their loving care and attention, 'suddenly flipped' after not getting the birthday present he wanted. The angry teenager apparently attacked anyone in sight, trashed the house, stole money then lunged at them with a carving knife and set fire to their car after dousing it with petrol. The man, still visibly distressed said, 'This is the thanks my partner and I get from a boy we have always done everything for with loving care. It is yet another tragic case of an adolescent with attitude biting the hand that feeds him. We will do all we can to forgive him and beg him to give himself in to the authorities.'

The boy remains at large, while police continue to make enquiries and search the area. If you see a youth fitting the following description, please contact the police immediately.

I read the description of me and wanted to scream. They used the two words that have plagued my life, as if that's the complete me and nothing else. Then I read the whole story again, screaming two other words. 'Loving care?' How could they write this stuff?

'Just look at me,' I said at last. 'Do I really look like a teenager on the rampage? OK, so I destroyed a car and what was in it. But the rest of that stuff is just rubbish. It's my uncle who's the maniac.'

I told them the whole story and hoped they wouldn't

think I was that terrible kid described in the news. They both hugged me and said they'd stick by me.

'I guess you think I should just tell the police the truth and let them sort everything,' I said. 'Well, it won't be that easy. Who's going to believe my side of the story? I'll get done for arson and be sent away. I want to lie low for a while and make sure Mum's okay before I have to face all that stuff. Will you help me?'

I was relieved they understood. 'The police told Gran to call them as soon as you show up,' Sophie said. 'She told them she would, but of course she won't. She said you need to climb over her fence from the builder's yard round the back, then you won't be seen. I think she's a bit excited about you being "wanted". She's always been a bit of a rebel herself. When she finds out what your uncle did to Merlin, I dread to think what she'll do to him.'

Lian gave me a birthday card and offered us homemade Chinese sweets.

'But let's not worry about all that stuff yet,' she announced. 'We're here to celebrate Fin's birthday, to wish his mum a speedy recovery and cherish my lovely friend Ella. I've got candles, food, music and games, so let's chill and enjoy.'

Much later, as it was getting dark, Lian looked out of the window at flames rising from the incinerator. 'He's burning stuff again. Bryn Griffiths is always burning stuff. I looked through the ashes earlier and found remains of a laptop, a phone and the wire frame of a suitcase. I bet they were Ella's. I'm sure someone cleared all her things out of this caravan and burnt the lot.'

'What about his dog?' I asked, peering outside. 'Is it still there? I can't see the poor thing.'

She handed me a pair of binoculars. 'Try these. Have a good look at what's going on over there. I dread to think what he's burning now.'

I stared at her red binoculars on a fluorescent yellow strap. I'd seen a pair just like them before. 'Where did you get those?' I asked.

She smiled. 'Off a guy in Edinburgh. Ella and I were on an assignment at uni and we wanted a pair for long distance surveillance, so we both bought exactly the same ones – bright red. I've never seen any like those anywhere else.'

'I have,' I said. 'I saw Bryn Griffiths with an identical pair when I met him that morning on the cliff path. He's got Ella's binoculars, I'm sure of it. He can't burn those, surely.'

I looked out of her window to the big caravan with the RECEPTION sign. The light was on inside so I could see clearly into it. A woman with short spiky bleached hair was standing at a table, peeling potatoes. I focused the binoculars and zoomed right in on her face, which was perfectly lit and easy to see. I watched very carefully as she lit a cigarette, blew out a cloud of smoke and began talking. After about a minute, I put down the binoculars and turned to Lian as calmly as I could.

'You'd better turn on the TV,' I told her. 'I've just discovered something.'

I didn't tell them exactly what I'd just seen. I was tired, confused and needed time to think carefully.

The television came on half-way through the local news. It was the end of the story I knew had just been told. It was official. The police had announced that the body found at Redsands Bay a week ago had now been identified from dental records as being Ella Brookes, a twenty-six-year-old journalist and part-time waitress, who died as a result of head injuries sustained from a fall – most likely onto rocks somewhere along the coast. There were no suspicious circumstances and her family had been informed.

We all looked at each other but said nothing. Eventually Lian asked me, 'Do you still think she was murdered and Bryn Griffiths was behind it, Fin?'

'He's certainly behind it, but I now think there's more to it than that.'

'It's funny you should say that. I've found out something at work that I want to tell you. You see … '

We all jumped at sudden knocking on the door. Lian stood nervously and crept over to open it. The tension grew as she slowly turned the handle and peered out into the night. We gasped with relief as Sophie's mum appeared. 'Taxi here. Time to take you home.'

'We've got to meet tomorrow,' I said urgently. 'There's more stuff to tell you. I've just had a thought and I need to check something out.'

Lian hugged us. 'Let's meet early afternoon. I finish work tomorrow at two o'clock. Meet back here, if you like – there's lots of food left.'

We left her alone in the little caravan, under which I pushed my bike, before we drove away chatting about the great time we'd had. Sophie's mum dropped me in the yard behind Mrs Boughtwood's back garden and waited till I was safely over the fence and indoors before she drove off.

Sophie's gran greeted me like a long-lost stray puppy and asked to know all that had happened. She wanted to call the police right then when I told her about Merlin, but I begged her not to.

'You poor thing,' she kept saying, as she touched the curtain to peep out into the street. 'I wouldn't be surprised if they're expecting you to be here and keeping an eye on us. We'll have to think of somewhere else to hide you till things calm down. In the meantime, you'd better have a good bath, dear. You look filthy.'

Before long I was clean, no longer smelling of banana sick, and curled up in bed. But it wasn't time for sleep yet. My brain was in overdrive and I had lots to think about. I was even more worried about Mum, as I hadn't heard back from her, so I knew she must be very ill. I googled 'pneumonia' and felt it was all my fault. I must have infected her with germs when I visited her. My screen said:

> 'Pneumonia, often caused by bacterial infection, is

an inflammation of the lungs and can be life-threatening, especially for those with serious underlying health conditions.'

With that guilt gnawing away at me, as well as blaming myself for what happened to Merlin, I felt really miserable and gloomy. I was scared, too, at having to tell the police what I'd just discovered about Ella's murder – especially as they described me as 'out of control' so probably wouldn't believe me anyway. I looked again at the online news report and read the description of me at the end. It was the same old label – the way everyone sees me. Special Educational Needs. I'd now have to show the world there was more to Finley than meets the eye. I was now over fourteen for a start: a teen on a mission. I was far from the teenage freak they described – and why did they finish with those two words to sum me up – the same old label they think explains everything?

Do not approach the boy, as he is not only very unpredictable but also profoundly deaf.

A quick note from Fin

To be honest, I never wanted to include this bit. I don't think it's that important, so I've put it here like this in case you want to skip it. Mrs Holmes reckons this will give a fuller picture of me, but I'm only mentioning my disability as it actually helped solve the murder mystery. Mind you, it wasn't necessary to mention it in the description of me in the news, as *if that's what makes me who I am. That really p***** me off. I don't really care being called deaf or hearing impaired, but I'm far more than that. I just want to be seen as me.*

You've probably already realised, as I've given enough clues, that I'm classed as 'profoundly deaf', which basically means I can hardly hear anything. I've got hearing aids (Mrs Holmes always made me wear them at school) which help me hear some sounds, but they're not great with speech and I hate wearing them. I prefer not to wear them at all at home and in the holidays. I'm actually quite happy with silence (not that it's TOTAL silence exactly).

Mrs Holmes says I shouldn't close myself off and live in my own bubble, but I told her that's often a happier place to be, as I prefer the world in my head than the world as it is – and anyway, I'm a Virgo so I'm okay with my own company! I knew that would make her tell me off – but she knows that hearing aids can make conversations where several people talk at once a real pain, which I describe as like trying to hear the world through frosted glass, if you get the drift. It's just so fuzzy and weird. I sometimes think my hearing aids are like horrible chunky glasses that make you see the world all distorted, like in those weird wobbly mirrors on the pier. To be honest, it's often easier to manage without them. I'd much rather lip-read, which I'm usually pretty good at. Most of the conversations I've written about were me speaking and lip-reading, but some were through signing. Mrs Holmes, Mum and Sophie often sign with me, but I usually prefer to communicate 'normally', even though I can get a bit lost sometimes (or totally confused when I'm tired).

I guess I was lucky that I learnt to speak before I went deaf. You see, I got meningitis when I was three and that basically zapped my hearing forever. Grandad told me that's when I nearly died and it was a terrible time for Mum, what with one thing and another. I think that's why she still worries about me a lot.

Anyway, I've always tried to manage and I reckon I do okay most days. They keep sending me to clinics and stuff, and are forever going on about cochlea implants, but sometimes I just want to be left alone to get on as best I can without the fuss. Adults don't always seem to understand me. Mrs Holmes does – she wasn't just the special needs co-ordinator at school but also a teacher of the hearing impaired, so I've got her to thank for lots. She's brilliant at signing and taught me some really disgusting words – which I find very useful when people annoy me. If I sign something obscene while smiling sweetly at the same time, no one suspects a thing. I haven't told Mrs Holmes that's what I do, so I might get in trouble when she finds out. It's worth the risk, I reckon! It's her idea for me to write my story and to tell the world what happened.

The thing I find a real pain is not being able to use a phone for talking and listening. That would be so cool and make life much easier. Then again, if I wasn't such a wiz at lip-reading, I would never have seen what Liz Baker and Bryn Griffiths were saying in secret inside their caravan. That's when I knew without doubt that Ella had been murdered and there was more to all this than I thought. It was also the reason why I had to take a massive risk.

Anyway, so now you know all that 'hearing impaired' stuff about me – if you didn't twig earlier. As far as I'm concerned, my deafness shouldn't make a difference to anyone else. It's certainly not going to stop me trying to become a vet, so there! So now you know – and Mrs Holmes will be happy I've given the 'back story', as she calls it. Basically I'm a kid who just happens to be deaf – but being deaf doesn't define who I am, no more than someone with a wart on their butt needs a label to tell the world they're a warted person who can't sit without fidgeting.

The last thing I want is people seeing what I can't do rather than who I am, or feeling sorry for me or treating me like some kind of weirdo. Sophie understands exactly and she says it's similar being in a wheelchair. People either ignore her completely or talk down to her like a toddler in a pushchair. We often say that when she's mayor and I'm chief vet of the world, we're going to change the universe – so all I can say is, WATCH OUT FOLKS!

FIFTEEN

I was shaken out of a deep sleep, wrapped in a blanket and dragged downstairs. My brain told me it was the middle of the night, but I could see it was just getting light as I was bustled out through the French windows and into the old air raid shelter in the back garden.

Mrs Boughtwood was in her dressing gown and gabbling at me as she led me down steps that were freezing on my bare feet.

'Sorry about all the drama, Finley. The police are at the front door. They've come to search the house. They're convinced you're lurking in the shadows and are about to set light to us all or stab us in our beds. It's best if we hide you in here while they have a good search then leave us alone. I'd better lock you in. Don't worry, you've got a couple of puppies in here for company. I'll be back for the all clear.'

I sat huddled in the gloom in a daze, just one small dusty window letting in pale pink light. The puppies licked my toes and played with anything I threw across the stone floor. I just hoped their yelps weren't too loud to give away my hiding place. When the door was pushed open, I blinked up, fearing the worst. Mrs Boughtwood stood smiling. 'I think we need a nice hot drink. It's safe to come indoors now. Danger over.'

Back in the kitchen, she looked more serious. 'It's just as well I locked you in the shelter with a padlock. You probably didn't hear the police trying the door to the shelter. Luckily he couldn't see in through the window. They thought you might be in the garage, too. They had a good search and upset all the cats, but I wouldn't be surprised if they come back. They think you smashed the dog at the front gate. It was broken open and the money stolen in the night. I'm upset about that – it's part of the family and we've had it for years.'

'That's terrible,' I said. 'I hope you don't think I did it.'

'Of course not, dear. But I wouldn't be surprised it was that ghastly uncle of yours. He's desperate to get hold of you and was ranting on my doorstep last night. He smelled of drink and was very aggressive. He made all sorts of threats.'

'I'm sorry,' I sighed. 'You've been really kind to me and I'm causing you hassle. If he and the police suspect I'm staying here, I need to move out.'

'But where will you go, dear?' She gave me one of her scary fixed smiles.

I shrugged, 'I'll think of somewhere.'

In fact, it was Sophie who came up with an answer. She pushed a key into my hand. 'Don't tell anyone, but I borrowed this from my other gran. She's got a beach hut down by the harbour. Number five. She never uses it, so you could use it if you want. You're not supposed to spend the night in it, but who's to know? It could be quite cosy with a sleeping bag and a few pillows. I'll organise those and a box of goodies. The hut is very tasteful inside. It's got a tap, a camping stove and a couple of candles, so what more do you want?'

'I want to look at your phone,' I said. 'I'd like to look more closely at your photos. You see, I've been thinking ... '

I told her what I had seen the night before in Bryn Griffiths' caravan. I was certain I'd seen Liz Baker talking about the discovery of Ella's body. I'd lip-read the lot. She'd said to him, 'You idiot. I told you to weigh down the body with stones. The police would never have found her if she was at the bottom of the sea.'

I showed Sophie some notes I'd scribbled – a sort of timeline I'd worked out:

Sunday 14th

Ella on cliff about midnight (low tide).

Falls/is pushed over edge.

Monday early morning

Body buried.

Bryn G seen later coming up cliff after finding Ella's binoculars.

Me witness.

Tuesday morning

High tide (05.53).

Getting light but no one about so speed boat able to come right up to cliff.

Body dug up and taken out to sea.

Few hours later I dig up shoulder bag, sandal and bracelet - body gone.

Friday

Our boat trip, maybe in same boat (ACE SHOT TRACKER)

Body found at Redsands Bay approx 72 hours after being thrown overboard - speed of travel along coast less than one mile per hour - very possible.

Sophie looked at me thoughtfully. 'Do you really think Ella's body had been in the same boat we were in a few days later?'

I reminded her that Mr Rattacheck had told us Bryn Griffiths sometimes borrowed his speedboat, so her photos of it were worth another look. She began flicking through images on her phone and giggled again at the ones of me getting soaked. When she got to the close-up of Mr Rattacheck's yachting shoes, I said, 'Enlarge that one and take a close look at the deck – look, by his left foot.'

As the picture grew before our eyes, we both stared in amazement. 'Are you thinking what I'm thinking?' I asked.

'It certainly looks like it. It's Ella's other earring. It

looks just like a little pearl heart, like the one in the photo Lian showed us.'

Although the enlarged picture was blurry, there seemed to be a shiny ring with what looked like a heart-shaped pearl, lodged between the planks of the deck. 'If that is really Ella's earring,' I said, 'surely it's proof she was murdered and her body was taken in that boat out to sea and dumped.'

'I don't think my fuzzy photo will convince the police of anything,' Sophie said.

'In that case, I'll have to collect the evidence myself. Traces of DNA could prove it was Ella's earring and if I use tweezers and a sterile bag to put it in, as well as photographs of the crime scene, then I reckon the police will have to investigate. I've fancied being a CSI officer since I had to dress up as one to see Mum.'

Sophie gave me a scary look. 'But you know what that means? We've got to break into the boat shed and find that earring without getting caught.'

'I think I know how,' I replied. 'I'll ask Lian to get the key to the boathouse. I know where it is.'

Sophie thought for a while before asking, 'Wouldn't it just be easier to ask Mr Rattacheck directly? He'd let us search his boat, surely.'

'Not if he knows something about the murder,' I winked cheesily. 'Rule number one of detective work: trust no one. I think I read that in a Scooby Doo book!'

The question '*Why* was Ella murdered?' was still in both our minds, and we should have thought about that more. Maybe then we would have avoided walking straight into danger and letting Lian follow directly in Ella's footsteps – right to the precipice.

When we got off the bus and arrived at her caravan, Lian was hyper and talking so fast I couldn't keep up. 'I think I've found out something about what Ella was investigating,' she gabbled excitedly. 'It was something to do with smuggling. I overheard someone at work whispering about 'Secret Sundays' and 'forbidden cargo' but then I found something last night in here after you left.'

She handed us a folded newspaper cutting. 'I found this tucked under the lino by the sink. I knew Ella would have left a clue somewhere. We were told when we were training together that whenever we work on secret or dangerous missions, it's wise to leave a hidden clue where you stay, just in case something goes wrong.'

I read the article, but I wasn't sure why Ella would have left it behind.

RUTHLESS GANGS SMUGGLE MIGRANTS IN LUXURY YACHTS

Organised gangsters are bribing owners of luxury yachts to carry illegal immigrants from the continent to the British Coast, according to reports.

Migrants desperate to reach the UK are paying to cross the channel from Brittany to the coast of England, landing in small ports and quiet fishing harbours unguarded by border agency staff.

Investigators in the Brittany capital Rennes are probing what they believe is a highly organised network of brutal criminals using ports on the north coast of Brittany for sending off yachts crammed with frightened immigrants. Demanding high fees while subjecting desperate refugees to appalling conditions, the gangs are thought to be part of a dangerous yet lucrative international people-trafficking trade.

Twenty frightened migrants without papers were recently found huddled in the cabin of a £100,000 yacht by Customs officers off the British Coast. The migrants said they had each paid 5,000 Euros to ruthless gang masters to reach the UK.

Scribbled across the bottom in felt pen was *Race at the Rocks to The Cask Creator*.

'Whatever does that writing mean?' I asked.

'I've got no idea,' Lian said. 'But it's definitely Ella's writing and, knowing her, I bet it's some sort of code.'

'In that case, I'd better get on the case,' Sophie chipped in, jotting down each word. 'I love working out word puzzles and secret messages.'

Lian showed us a webpage. 'I've looked at this stuff from the National Crime Agency. It says how small ports and marinas are being targeted by people-smugglers and organised criminals. I reckon Ella was on to something round here, but I haven't been able to find a recorded message. We were trained to keep audio diaries as back-up. In the old days reporters used to speak into Dictaphones to record their comments, but we now use USB voice recorders. Ella's must have been burnt with all her other stuff.'

I suddenly remembered the memory stick I'd found the day before at the bottom of the cliff, so I snatched it from my pocket.

'You mean like this?' I asked, waving it excitedly under her nose. She snatched it from me eagerly, immediately plugged it into her laptop and loaded the audio file.

'It's only a small file,' she said, 'but I'll play it and hope for the best.'

I watched the screen and saw the little indicator button move across the bottom as the sound played, not that I could hear a thing. Both Sophie and Lian reacted, so I knew something important was happening. When it stopped playing, Lian turned to me with tears in her eyes. 'Hearing Ella's voice again is just so wonderful – but it's the last thing she ever said before she fell to her death.'

'What does she say?' I was desperate to know.

'We'll play it again and I'll sign for you,' Sophie said. 'It's Ella speaking and she says: "It's Sunday 14th August, about midnight. I'm up on the cliff and scanning the sea. The tide has just started coming in and I can see through my binoculars the sandbank at the mouth of the estuary is starting to disappear under white-topped waves. There's enough moonlight to see across the river and, yes … I can see a dark shape moving in on the tide. It's heading towards the cove and if I'm not mistaken its Race at the

Rocks. My plan is to check out the inn as soon as it's light, then I'll finally be able to … sorry? What are you saying?" '

Lian broke in, 'At this point there are lots of muffled noises. We can hear someone shouting and ranting, then there's a sort of thud and a scream. Lots of weird crackles and bumps before it all goes quiet.' She wiped her eyes. 'It's all very upsetting, but it proves she didn't jump. Someone attacked her and pushed her off the cliff, I'm sure of it.'

'In that case, you can take it to the police and they'll have to investigate,' Sophie said.

'The only trouble is,' Lian added, looking doubtful, 'audio recordings are notoriously difficult to prove as authentic in court. They can so easily be faked and I've never known a criminal case to rely on them alone. I think it's a brilliant lead for us as it proves Ella was on to something – I guess to do with smuggling, but that recording alone doesn't prove she was killed or who did it. There aren't any clear voices, just a lot of screeching. It isn't Bryn Griffiths' voice at the end.'

I interrupted. 'In that case, I definitely need to find Ella's earring in that boat to prove she was dumped at sea. There could be other evidence inside ACE SHOT TRACKER as well. This is where I need your help, Lian.'

I explained about the earring in the speedboat and when she looked at Sophie's photo, she was even more certain than us that it was Ella's.

'You're right, Fin,' she began excitedly. 'If we can establish that Ella's body was in that speedboat, we'll prove she didn't jump or fall by accident and that somebody must have killed her and tried to hide the evidence. What can I do to help, Fin?'

I told her I needed the key to the boathouse. 'It's on a hook behind the reception desk where you work. The key's got a red tag and the hook is on the top row of hooks near to a shelf. If I can have it for ten minutes, I'll be able to get a copy cut just round the corner at the hardware store. I'd like to sneak in the boathouse when no one's about and take my time.'

'And me,' Sophie insisted. 'You don't think I'd let you take such a risk on your own, do you? Besides, I'll be your photographer to record everything properly.'

'I'm back at work at eight o'clock tomorrow morning, so I'll get the key for you then,' Lian smiled. 'What a team we make. Tomorrow will be a safe time to look at the boat, as Mr Rattacheck works all day at his other hotel on a Saturday and Bryn Griffiths works away at the weekend. They're the only two who use the speedboat. I already found out about that.' She looked out of the window to the field next to the caravan park. 'Did you notice a cattle truck in that field yesterday? It's not there now. I heard it chugging off early this morning before it was light. Bryn Griffiths was driving it. So I asked a few people at work this morning about him. They all know who he is, but no one seems to like him. Apparently he's always away every Friday till late, then he's off again early Saturday till after midnight every Sunday. So, if that's the case, he couldn't have killed Ella at midnight on Sunday. But here's the other weird thing – they all said how Bryn Griffiths fancied Ella and used to flirt with her like mad. Knowing Ella, she used her charms to get information out of him, but it's made me wonder if he wouldn't have done her any harm. Now I've heard that recording, I'm sure he wasn't there as his loud voice would be easy to hear.'

I nodded as I looked back outside at his dog tethered by the incinerator. Somehow I wasn't surprised by what Lian had said, as it fitted in with one of my theories. Ideas were fitting into place in my mind, but I knew the tricky bit was to find proof and convince the world about what I thought had happened that Sunday night nearly two weeks before.

The beach hut was painted inside and out in vertical stripes; duck-egg blue and ice-white. Inside were two stripy canvas chairs, cushions printed with seagulls, a shelf with cups, plates, matches and candles, and a little sink with draining board. I told Sophie this was the height of luxury after sleeping in the garden shed. With the doors hooked back, the evening sun poured in and danced on the ceiling, reflecting off the water just down the beach. All manner of boats bobbed in the harbour on the incoming tide, as a police launch headed across the estuary – so I quickly fastened the doors shut.

The windowless beach hut was really dark inside, so I lit a candle and switched on a string of LED fairy lights. The familiar smells of timber, the sea and a flickering candle gave this place a feeling of snug security, despite the police searching for me just beyond the closed doors.

The only downside of my new home was the lack of Wi-Fi, so I couldn't email Mum or read her blog. Instead, I sent her a text to tell her I was fine and to ask how she was. Her reply was not what I wanted to see:

> Fin, I am worried about you. Where are you? I am still feeling weak and feeble but battling on. I need to see you. Calvin keeps phoning. I have a piece of paper to sign about you. Guess I have to. Love Mum x

My heart sank. Surely Uncle Calvin wasn't getting her to sign another document so soon. That was all I needed. I quickly texted back.

> Don't sign anything. I'll come and see you soon. This weekend – not sure when. Things to do but don't worry about me. Fin.

After buying fish and chips from the end of the quay, I locked myself in the beach hut to eat them. Sitting on a canvas chair, I went over things in my mind and tried to plan for the next day. It was a struggle as I felt so sleepy and it was difficult to think straight. After attempting to wash my greasy fingers in cold water in a tiny sink, I put on a jumper and slid into the sleeping bag. Snuffing out the candle, I lay looking into solid darkness, expecting to lie awake and think a lot more. But it didn't happen like that. I fell asleep almost instantly – until panic struck in the middle of the night.

SIXTEEN

Somewhere in my dream I could hear music – just like I used to be able to hear it. I heard every single note as Sophie played a pink grand piano in a world nothing like the one I knew. All of a sudden we were both running barefoot down the beach to the sound of waves breaking on the shore, where Mum and Grandad were dancing and laughing. Mum was well and happy, Grandad could see us and waved cheerily, as Masie played with Merlin and Uncle Calvin at the water's edge. It was a perfect sunny day and, as I stopped to balance stones like giant pearls in shimmering towers, I saw a cameraman filming us from a small boat out at sea. Although I couldn't see his face, I knew he was my dad. Everyone was smiling, the music was awesome and the sea sparkled in the sun … till Uncle Calvin was stung by a giant jelly fish and suddenly snarled, with red eyes and drooling fangs, as he lunged at me with a clawed fist. Dragging me into the water, he shoved my face under the waves as I tried desperately to scream for help. My cold body was sucked downwards – down, down into freezing darkness. I was drowning as my life was flashing before my stinging eyes …

I woke with my heart thumping and my body soaked. I was lying in cold water, my sleeping bag and pillow drenched, and the darkness so intense that I was terrified. I had no idea where I was and for many seconds I'm sure I was screaming. Not able to find a light, I crawled through water, trying to grope a way out of my nightmare. As I began to realise where I might be, I fumbled my way around the beach hut, pulled myself to my feet and paddled into a solid wooden wall. Scrabbling around in the terrifying blackness, I eventually found a catch, turned it and pushed open one of the doors. Water poured out over my bare feet and a sea breeze cut through my soaked clothes. Streetlights further down the quay shone across the beach and rebooted my brain – so I was now able to recognise landmarks and orientate myself, sensing at last where I was. My head continued throbbing in surges of confusion and fear.

A pale wash of light now dribbled into the beach hut, so I was able to find the switch to the fairy lights strung across the ceiling. Their glow reflected up from the swirling water at my feet and it was only then it dawned on me what I had done. The tap was still running into the sink where I'd used a plug when washing my hands before bed.

I hadn't turned the tap off properly, so water had been spilling out over the floor for the last few hours. Being unable to hear it and blissfully locked in my dream world, I had no idea I was flooding the place and soaking all my stuff. The shock of waking like that, being so disorientated and scared, took a long time to get over. So did mopping out the beach hut and trying to make it decent again. That meant keeping the doors open so I could bail it out, and I felt vulnerable that anyone could see me, even though the world out there seemed empty. That was till I saw movement out on the water.

Dark though it was, I knew the man rowing a small dinghy across the harbour between bobbing yachts moored in the rising tide was Bryn Griffiths. His torch-lit shape and the way he moved convinced me it was him, but so did the muzzled pit bull terrier peering over the side of his boat. By now it was after two o'clock in the morning and I was intrigued to know where he was heading and why. I put on my trainers to head off along the beach to follow him, and was surprised when he pulled up alongside a large white boat that looked like a stylish top-of-the-range cruiser. His torch flashed over the hull as he climbed aboard, pushing his dog up ahead of him. In a split-second of dancing torchlight, the last word from the name of the boat leapt out at me. I needed to make sure I wasn't mistaken.

Heading further along the beach, I walked out on the sandbank that separated the estuary from the open sea. I sat down at the furthest point, close to the water's edge beside the channel where the cruiser would have to pass if it set out to sea. Sure enough, after a few minutes the anchor rose, a motor churned the water and the classy boat began to move slowly from its mooring, towing the dinghy behind it. As it passed close by me, a glow from the outer harbour lights brushed over its bow and I saw the boat's full name: RACE AT THE ROCKS. Now I knew another piece of the jigsaw had just snapped into place. The murder mystery was slowly beginning to unravel.

Saturday morning was a long time coming. Cold, wet and unable to sleep, I tried to dry out my phone but I just couldn't get it to work. As the sky eventually lightened over the sea, I hung my sleeping bag over the beach hut doors, hoping it would dry in the breeze, and I walked into town to wait for a café to open. Being Bank Holiday weekend, the main street began to open for business early, so at last I was able to sit in the Seagull Café with a steaming plate of beans on toast as well as my steaming socks, trainers and a row of ten pound notes on a radiator. I sat away from the window just in case a patrol car happened to be passing. Even so, I could see across the street to a newsagent where a billboard announced in large letters: VIOLENT YOUTH STILL AT LARGE. Catching my reflection in the glass, I had to smile that the violent youth staring back at me looked more like a pathetic drowned rat who didn't have the energy to hurt a fly.

By nine o'clock the street was bustling and I could walk around without feeling as if a bright orange arrow was pointing at me saying IT'S HIM. I stood outside The Actor's Creak, where Sophie joined me with a comment that said it all. 'It looks like you had a rough night.'

'You should have seen me before I scrubbed up in a café washroom.' I didn't tell her how I'd flooded her gran's beach hut, as I might have been kicked out and I hoped to stay in it for a few more nights.

Lian appeared beside us and pressed a key in my hand. 'Is this what you're waiting for?' she smiled. 'Just to warn you – Mr Rattacheck is in his office this morning, but don't worry, he didn't see me take the key.'

'Give it to me and I'll get a copy cut,' Sophie interrupted. 'My dad knows the key-cutter guy so I'll get it done without any questions. You're too famous, Fin. You were on the news again this morning.'

I gave her one of my damp ten pound notes and within minutes she was back with a smile and a new key. Lian took the original back to its usual place so no one would be any the wiser. Sophie and I could now take our time searching the boat without fearing someone would discover the key was missing.

As it was regatta weekend, the harbour was already busy with all sorts of boats being scrubbed and smartened-up, the Canoe Club practising for races and marshals setting out buoys for raft competitions. Many of the boathouses had their doors open, with gleaming bows nudging out onto the sand. So when we opened up the boathouse with the red doors, no one took any notice of us cautiously peering inside. Sophie left her wheelchair round the back and used her sticks for slipping inside inconspicuously – from bright sunshine on the quayside into deathly darkness where the speedboat stretched lifeless under a tarpaulin.

'It's like a corpse wrapped in a shroud in the morgue,' she said. 'It's so cold and spooky. Just as well I brought a decent torch.'

She switched it on as I pulled the door shut and our shadows whirled creepily across the sagging timber roof. Her camera flash bounced off oily creosoted beams as she gave a running commentary into the memory stick hanging round her neck. I pulled back part of the tarpaulin so we could step into the front of the boat from a wooden platform beside it. When we were both inside, I pulled the tarpaulin back over us so we could scrabble around under it, like being in a tent. Sophie's torch beam swept across the deck around the driver's seat, while I crawled under the dashboard to examine nooks and crannies on the floor. I didn't like the thought that Ella's body must have been lying right there before she was thrown over the side.

Suddenly I saw a glint in the torchlight – a tiny speck of silver wedged in the decking under the passenger's seat. I knew immediately this was what we were looking for. Sophie took close-up photos, spoke into the recorder then passed me a small plastic bag, surgical gloves and tweezers. I carefully teased out the earring and, making sure I only touched it with tweezers, I sealed it in the bag. We had the evidence we needed to prove Ella hadn't just fallen into the sea. I was about to give Sophie a high-five when she grabbed my hand and mouthed, 'There's someone there. The door's open.'

She flicked off her torch and we scrambled to the back of the boat in the pitch black. There was a strong oily smell and the floor was damp as we squeezed behind the back seats, being careful not to knock against a petrol can. The boat rocked and light spilled in as the tarpaulin was wrenched back past the front seats. We couldn't see who was there as they clambered around the boat. Their feet were scarily close to my fingers – shoes with black and white checks. Not daring to move, I could only wait for Sophie to let me know when it was safe to stir. I felt the boat move as the tarpaulin was pulled back to where it had been. When Sophie's torch switched on again and she gave the thumbs-up, we gave a sigh of relief and scrambled out. She told me what she'd heard.

'That was Mr Rattacheck and one of his staff. Those boxes they put on the back seat are fireworks for Monday night. He said they're letting them off from this boat in the harbour at the end of the regatta. They had no idea we were here so ... '

'What's up?' I asked, as I helped her climb out of the boat.

'I left one of my sticks by the door. I forgot all about it – luckily they didn't see it. I wouldn't want to upset the nice Mr Rattacheck.'

Back out in the sunlight I could see Sophie's face and talk more easily.

'I reckon Mr Rattacheck is cool,' I told her. 'I bet he's

got no idea Liz Baker attacked Ella on the cliff. And I reckon Bryn Griffiths is involved in crime – like some sort of smuggling. I saw him very early this morning taking a massive powerboat out to sea. Guess what it was called.'

Sophie smiled. 'I bet it was one of those names Ella wrote on that newspaper cutting. *Race at the Rocks* or T*he Cask Creator*.

'Hey, you're right. It's the first one. I've got no idea what the second one is.'

'Nor me. But I know both of them are owned by Mr Rattacheck.'

I laughed. 'How can you possibly know that?'

She grinned, looking very pleased with herself. 'They're just like the speedboat – Ace Shot Tracker. And just like The Actor's Creak. They're all anagrams of Eros Rattacheck. He owns all of them. I think they're all tied up with Ella in some way. She knew about them – that's why she left the clues.'

I patted her on the back. 'Not bad, chief inspector. So what's *The Cask Creator* all about, then?'

'That's my next line of enquiry, Constable. Just give me a few more hours and I'll crack it. In the meantime, shouldn't we take that earring to the police right now?'

'Well *I* can't, can I? As soon as I show up, they'll nab me. I think it's best if Lian deals with it. They're more likely to listen to her.'

We knew Lian would be pleased to take our evidence to the police as soon as she left work at two o'clock. I kept checking the earring was safe inside my pocket as we headed along the seafront, bought hotdogs and fought our way through dive-bombing seagulls back to the beach hut. I was glad to find it and my sleeping bag much drier than when I'd left.

Sophie said it smelt a bit damp, but I changed the subject and asked if I could use her phone to see Mum's latest blog.

> Saturday
> I've now had days of chest X-rays and CT scans, and at last it seems my infections are responding to antibiotics. I still feel tired, wheezy and grotty but I'm pleading with my neutrophils to grow and fight back.
>
> I'm woken up around 01.30 each morning for blood pressure checks etc. – then again at 6am. Yesterday my head started to feel hot and sore and by last night my hair was coming out. This wasn't so much in clumps but just getting thinner and 'letting go'. Although not pleasant, this was expected. I know this is temporary and my hair will grow back – maybe a different colour and texture. Until then I'll try the wig to show I'm putting up a fight. Yes, I'm doing my best to put on a brave face, even though they tell me I'll be here much longer than they expected. Grrr.
>
> The staff are brilliant and we try to laugh when we can.
>
> I haven't had chance to talk to Fin yet but

I've got a piece of paper for us to sign. The good news is – his stem cells are a perfect match, so they say he could be a donor if he still wants to be – bless him! I'm desperate to see him – we so need to talk. I'm hopeful he and I will emerge stronger as a result of all this palaver. I've never been much good with patience, but I'm learning fast.

Love to all, Ali

'Yes! That's just magic – I can be a donor after all,' I yelled, punching the air. I told Sophie how my phone was dead and I could no longer contact Mum, but I was determined now to go and see her.

Sophie looked serious. 'It's high risk if you go to the hospital. The police are bound to be looking for you there. They've even been to our house. Gran said they keep calling there too, as they're convinced you're hiding in her garage. She found your uncle snooping around her garden and had to chase him off by waving a frying pan.'

I laughed at the thought of him getting beaten up by Mrs Boughtwood, but realised she was right. Being 'wanted' meant I had to be careful. 'I guess I need to disguise myself a bit more.'

'Then maybe we should pay a visit to a charity shop and get you a new image. Time for a make-over, Fin.'

I drew the line at buying a burka or niqab, which Sophie tried to persuade me to try on. 'No one will know it's you,' she insisted.

'Yeah, but *I* will. I'll settle for a baseball cap and a hoodie.' I left the shop wearing both and a pair of shades. Even so, I felt everyone was staring at me as I pushed Sophie's wheelchair along the street.

'You could always sit in here,' she said. 'No one ever takes any notice of me when I'm in one of these.'

We waited at the entrance to the pier, where we'd arranged to meet Lian. With so many people about, we thought we'd missed her when she hadn't appeared by half past two. Sophie gave her a call but there was no answer, so we headed over to The Actor's Creek. We guessed the holiday weekend was making things extra busy in the restaurant. Just as we got there, I saw a woman getting in the driving seat of a red sports car then shooting off towards the cliff road.

'Someone's in a hurry,' I remarked casually. 'She looked like Liz Baker.'

'I'll go in to find Lian,' Sophie said. 'It's probably best if you stay out of the way just in case your disguise doesn't work.'

While I was waiting in the street, a police car came out of a side road and drove very slowly towards me. With my head down and shoulders hunched, I hurried into the nearest doorway. I waited inside the shop, pretending to browse a stand of postcards, with quick glances out through the window as the car drove past, before I turned to see two familiar women staring at me from behind the counter. It was only then I realised I was in the Tourist Information Centre.

'Hello, Finley. Everything all right? We've just seen your Mum's blog,' Sandra smiled. 'Not an easy time, love. Good about your stem cells, hey? Nice that you've got some to spare. We sold all your cards, by the way. They went like hot cakes, didn't they, Marjorie?'

The other woman looked petrified, as if I was about to self-combust, and she seemed incapable of speaking. I was lost for words as well, but heard myself mutter, 'Any messages for Mum when I see her next?'

I'm not sure what they answered. What with trying to lip-read through sunglasses, while taking quick peeps out of the window, I lost the thread of what they were both saying at once, but I could see Marjorie's hand slowly reaching for a phone. As the police car had driven on, I made my way to the door with a quick wave. 'Thanks then – bye' and I ran to find Sophie, who was sitting outside the revolving doors to The Actor's Creak. I knew instantly something was wrong.

'Where's Lian?' I asked.

'Gone. She handed in her notice at midday and left – back to Glasgow.'

'That can't be true,' I blurted.

'That's what I told them,' she sighed, 'But Mr Rattacheck insisted. He wasn't very happy about it either – moaning that another member of staff had let him down.'

We both knew Lian would never leave without telling us. I told Sophie to keep trying her phone while I'd go to her caravan. As I'd left my bike under it, I needed to go and collect it, and I hoped to find Lian there. I headed to the bus stop and called back to Sophie, 'See you later – this evening at your gran's.'

The bus driver gave me a long, hard stare. I took my ticket and went straight to the back seat, keeping my head down before turning to look out of the window with my hood up, all the way up the winding cliff road. When the bus reached the caravan park, I stood and went to the doors, but they didn't open. I was the only one wanting to get off and the driver was making some kind of announcement to everyone. I quickly thumped the doors' emergency button and, as they juddered open, I leapt off and ran to the cliff path where I skidded down and ducked out of sight. I waited in the undergrowth for a few minutes before climbing back up to the road. The bus had gone, so I quickly made my way up the track towards Lian's caravan.

Smoke was billowing across the field where the cattle truck was parked. As I got closer, I could see flames rising from the incinerator, black smoke wafting over a red sports car nearby. When I got to Lian's caravan I saw the door was open, so I called, 'Hi, Lian.'

Almost immediately a face appeared – Liz Baker's. She was in overalls and rubber gloves. 'She's gone. Left this place in a right mess.'

'Can you tell me where she's gone?' I asked. She had a cigarette in her mouth, which made lip-reading tricky.

'No idea. Off you go. I've got work to do.'

'Can I get my bike? I left it under here.'

Her eyes glared. 'You're that kid. The one they're after. Get out of here.'

I began pulling my bike from under the caravan, then looked up at her. She was watching something down on the road. 'That's a police siren,' she said. 'They must know you're here. They're at the cliff path, so go quick or I'll tell them you're up here.'

'Then I'll tell them about you,' I answered, surprising myself at what I was saying. 'And about what you did to Ella.'

At first I thought she was going to lunge at me with a mop. Her face looked like thunder. 'I don't know what or who you're talking about, so bugger off.'

I got on my bike and backed away as I played my trump card. It was a risk, but if I got a reaction I'd know my hunch was right.

'We know you dumped her in the sea from the speedboat. We've got evidence. You'd better not harm Lian. We know everything.'

The mop hit my front wheel and a scrubbing brush hit my cycle helmet. I'd learned enough. Whatever she was shouting at me, I didn't stay to find out, but sped off down the track, onto the cliff road where an empty police car was parked in a lay-by, so I pedalled like mad all the way back to town.

Cycling round the back of Mrs Boughtwood's house, I propped my bike against the fence then climbed onto the crossbar so I could clamber over and drop into her garden. Before I could get over the top, a hand grabbed my ankle.

Losing my hold on the fence, I fell to the ground by my bike, cracking my cycle helmet on the handlebars and knocking the bike over on top of me. The next thing I knew, the bike was being yanked off me and a hand was at my throat. It dragged me to my feet and, just as I blinked into Uncle Calvin's enraged eyes, his fist slammed in my face and I crumpled onto the gravel. Just able to roll away from a kick to my chin, I scrambled onto my knees only to get a knee in my neck and down I went again, slamming my face on the fence and tasting blood on my lips. Dazed and spitting a mouthful of grit, I felt hands grab my shoulders and pull me up again, gripping both my sleeves. I quickly wrenched my arms out of my hoodie and slipped free. Uncle Calvin fell backwards and sprawled into a pile of pallets, still grasping my hoodie. I turned, grabbed my bike and threw it at him. The front wheel slammed into his nose and he crashed onto his back, both hands clutching his nosebleed as pallets flew in all directions. I turned and ran, and with one leap hauled myself up the fence, flipped over the top and landed in the bushes. Without looking back, I darted down the garden to the back door, hurled myself through it, slammed it shut and bolted it quickly. As I turned, panting and bleeding, I realised Mrs Boughtwood was standing in the kitchen with broken plates at her feet and she was screaming.

The next thing I knew, I was sitting in the front room with my cycle helmet being unstrapped and Sophie dabbing at my face with a damp flannel. The warm water in her bowl turned from pink to red as she kept dipping the flannel and squeezing it. Apart from a throbbing cheek and feeling a bit sick, I didn't think I was too bad, but Sophie's gran said I looked dreadful. 'Your face is a mess, Finley. That man can't get away with this. It's time to call the police and sort this out once and for all. We can't go on like this.'

Sophie tried to argue with her. 'No, Gran. They'll take Fin away. We just need a bit longer to find Lian and let Fin see his Mum. First of all they need to know about the evidence we've found.'

I suddenly realised I no longer had it. 'It's in my hoodie – he tore it off me.'

Her gran wouldn't change her mind. 'Then I have to call the police right now. That man is a monster and must be stopped. There's no telling what he'll do.'

She left the room and I whispered to Sophie. 'I can't stay here. I'll go to the beach hut. Meet me there midday tomorrow when I get back from the hospital. I need to work out what to do next.'

'Me too,' Sophie answered anxiously. 'I'll need to tell you what I've found out. I've just solved another of Ella's puzzles. This is getting scary, so take care, Fin.' She wiped my face with the flannel again then kissed my cheek. 'Your face doesn't look great right now – but I still think you're brilliant. Hashtag my hero.'

I sneaked from the room and hoped her gran wouldn't hear me as I tiptoed down the hall and out through the front door. It was getting dark but the air was still warm and I was thinking I didn't even need the hoodie, when I spotted a white car pulling away from the kerb down the road and slowly coming towards me, its headlights on full.

Instinctively, I leapt over the front gate, darted across the road and down an alley into a park. I kept running, past children's swings and over a skateboard park. Glancing back as I dodged a kid on rollerblades, I saw the car parked at the end of the alley with its doors opening. With a frantic sprint, I headed off down another alley, up a hill past holiday flats, over the main road and into East Cliff Gardens. From here I could follow the coastal path leading down to the promenade and back to the pier.

Lights from the arcades were blazing and flashing, with crowds milling around the entrance to the travelling funfair, so I could mingle and stroll past unnoticed. Who would possibly care about a kid in a muddy T-shirt, with a bashed face stopping to buy a hamburger at a kiosk on the seafront?

Feeling confident I wasn't being followed, I walked around the fairground trying not to squeal as I ate salty chips with a split lip. Then, leaving the crowds behind, I headed down to the beach and jogged round to the quayside. When I arrived at the beach hut, I unlocked the door, slipped inside, switched on the lights and pushed the door shut. Safe at last – at least, for a while, I thought.

Still breathless, I lay back on a slightly damp sleeping bag and pillow, relieved I'd made it back in one piece, but more concerned about Lian. I was sure she could be in real danger and, although I now felt fairly safe myself tucked away in a locked beach hut, I was only too aware it might not be for much longer.

SEVENTEEN

As if things weren't bad enough, feeling so cut off from everything and everyone, I now had a dead watch. It just wouldn't work – either because of delayed damp or from the bashing by Uncle Calvin. So when I pushed open the beach hut doors on Sunday morning to greet the world, I had no idea what time it was. From the brightness of the sun and the number of people on the quayside, I guessed it was later than I'd imagined.

My plan was to find out train times at the railway station, then go to the hospital during the morning. As I walked through town, I glanced up at the church clock and was amazed to see it was quarter to eleven. Breaking into a sprint, I approached the station but stopped suddenly when I saw two police cars parked outside and police talking to people at the entrance.

Had I known what was posted online at the time, I would have been horrified and taken more care.

RUNAWAY TEEN STRIKES AGAIN

Police are intensifying their search for a fourteen-year-old boy accused of arson and assault, who is thought to be sleeping rough in the town. Mr Calvin Gibson, the boy's uncle, was again attacked last evening when he tried to offer his nephew help. Mr Gibson, who has a heart condition and is unable to work, sustained a broken nose when attempting to prevent his nephew from breaking into property in Braxted Avenue. A local resident called for police assistance but the youth ran away before he could be apprehended. Mr Gibson received emergency treatment at the scene and is said to be severely traumatised and is being cared for by his partner, also an invalid. Various sightings of the youth have been reported and the public should inform the police of the whereabouts of anyone thought to be the young suspect.

I headed back to the seafront to see if I could catch a bus instead. More police. The only escape route was to dart onto the pier and hope to hide among all the kids playing on slot machines or gathered round the Superbike Simulator. I blended in reasonably well, as no one seemed to take any notice of me. Everyone was absorbed in trying to score points or win their fortunes on machines that coughed out coins like silver vomit.

I strolled on through the arcade, past the Addams

Family Electric Shock Machine, go karts driven by manic toddlers around a tiny track, a party of foreign students getting excited at an air hockey table, couples giggling at the Talking Love Meter, random lone gunmen trying to win a cuddly toy on Professor Coggins' Shooting Gallery, then out onto the pier deck itself. I watched a girl rolling a coin down the Black Hole, which was like a well with a funnel inside and a tiny coin-sized hole a short way down it, with a sign: 'Spin a coin to eternity and watch it keep rolling into oblivion'. If I could have fitted down it, I'd have been tempted to escape into oblivion myself.

Far ahead, at the end of the pier, men sat with fishing rods and tins of bait. Having done the same a few times, I headed towards them to see what they were catching. Their lines stretched off into the swirling grey-green sea, white-topped and changing to sparkling blue whenever the sun broke through clouds. A boy who lived opposite us was reeling in a mackerel and he turned to give me a thumbs-up, then looked away to reach in his bag. Before going over, I turned to look back along the seawall and the line of cliffs, where I spotted a yellow and black helicopter hanging above the lifeboat station like an unwelcome wasp at a picnic. I couldn't hear it, or anything, as I watched this busy, silent world of a coastal bank holiday weekend; buzzing but soundless. Like a TV permanently stuck on mute, my window on life seemed in that moment more remote, disconnected and lonely than ever. Everyone was out having fun – but not in my world anymore, and I felt thoroughly miserable. I looked across to the bench where

Mum and I sat the week before, laughing at our soaking in the sunset, and my spirits sank even lower.

Even though I could smell the sea, I heard no waves, nor the breeze blowing in my ears. The vibrating planks at my feet told me the sea below was restless and I peered down through a gap into the rolling water, then across to the sandbank close by, only exposed at low tide, now with families paddling around the edge; smiling, happy and together. Lucky them.

Raising my eyes towards the cliff road, I caught a flash of red racing down towards the promenade. If I'd had binoculars, I'd have fixed them on what I had no doubt was Liz Baker's sports car heading into town. Instead, I went to a telescope fixed near the end of the pier, fed it a coin and spun it round to sweep the shoreline. With my eye pressed against the eyepiece, I moved the magnified circle of light along the beach and up to the road. Then, by scanning left and right, I tried to find the sports car in all the traffic. Nothing. The scenes and people I spied through that single circular frame were completely unaware of my prying eye skimming along the coast road towards the estuary. It was only then, as I zoomed in on the distant bridge, that I caught a flash of red in the sunlight – speeding over the water to the cliffs beyond. In that flash, I realised what must be happening. Suddenly, through the lens of that telescope, I glimpsed another piece of the jigsaw slotting into place – and I knew I had to go to where that car was heading.

Lowering the telescope, I swept the lens across hotel

rooftops in a blur of tiles and windows, then down to the arcade roof on the pier. My little round window on the world hovered over the Black Hole before finally focussing on a face beside it, staring straight at me and mouthing, 'There's the brat.'

At first I thought it was a bizarre trick of the telescope as I glimpsed Uncle Calvin striding towards me, a phone to his ear before the image went black. My time was up – but not just on the telescope as the money ran out. I knew I was cornered and the hunter was closing in on his prey. In a sickening turn of fate, he'd appeared at the worst time and place, just when I had nowhere to run. How had he known I was here?

With a quick glance behind me to the end of the pier, in the hope that one of the fishermen would come to my rescue, I saw the boy neighbour with his phone pointing at me. He was cheerfully giving Uncle Calvin a wave. So that answered my question. Some sort of Neighbourhood Watch scheme was tracking down the evil fire-raiser of Hillside Road.

For a man who described himself as having a heart condition, Uncle Calvin was charging towards me looking not only super-fit but super-mad. His face was bloated, sweaty, the nose swollen and bruised. For a millisecond I thought about running at him, dodging past, then sprinting away off the pier – but there wasn't room to give him a wide enough berth without the risk of a rugby tackle or a swipe from his fist. He'd easily strike me to the ground for the beating of my life. Instead, I backed away to the end of the pier, but soon realised I was stuck between the devil and the deep blue sea – literally.

If I didn't act in seconds, Uncle Calvin could pounce; he was now just strides away. With my back pressed against the pier railings and nothing but churning ocean beyond, I had a stark choice: oblivion or a serious public beating-up. At least oblivion offered a tad more mystery and excitement … so I jumped.

I'm not sure how I did it – it all happened so fast. One second I was facing an advancing predator hurling abuse, the next I'd clambered over the railings and dropped, grabbing the bottom of the rails and clinging on for dear life as my legs dangled over the sea. I swung my feet, trying to throw myself onto a girder under the pier so I could pull myself across beams towards the shore like a swinging orang-utan. Instead, I dropped, grabbed at an iron bar and hung for only seconds. My hands slipped on slimy seaweed and I fell.

As soon as I hit the cold water and plunged down and down into what I was sure was oblivion, I feared I would never surface again. Anger tore through me – why ever did it have to end like this?

They say drowning is the best way to die, quietly letting go and slipping into nothingness. That didn't happen – there was no gentle slipping into anything. I just kept spinning, sinking into a spiralling void, swirling round and down, round and down. My hands groped at the churning water, clawing madly in the desperate hope of grabbing anything – anything to pull me up into air, as my lungs burned and heaved for a gulp of precious oxygen.

As I sank deeper, I fought with sapping strength to get my mouth above water to suck in just one breath. That's when my head filled with sounds. My silent world burst with an explosion of voices ... crashing music ... rumbling drums ... and my own heart beat, like throbbing thunder. I think I was screaming, too – if you can scream underwater.

I now know what utter panic feels like ... as it gave way to hopeless despair. The voice was no more than a distant whisper at first. It was calling me and seemed to come from a warm glow, like liquid flame in the deep green darkness. It was as if Grandad was telling me to fight back. 'Don't give up.' Although I hadn't heard his voice since I was three, I knew it was him whispering in my ear, urging me to keep going. There was still unfinished business up there.

Choking saltwater rushed down my nose and throat. My clothes filled like a sponge and dragged me further below the waves ... down ... down ... down. But I fought. I fought like mad. I *had* to live – to climb back to the surface, to sunlight, to the life I wasn't ready to lose. Not yet. I wasn't going to give up. For Grandad's sake. For Mum's sake. For Ella's sake. For mine.

I could feel myself being dragged by a current, so I kicked, straightened my body and shook off my trainers. As I tried to tread water, I felt myself rising at last. I could see pale daylight far above, so I reached up to it and thrashed my outstretched legs. The strain of kicking sucked from my limbs what little energy I had left – but I rose and finally broke the surface with a triumphant gasp.

Amazingly, I had drifted under the pier to the other side from where I'd fallen. The pillars stretching above me looked massive but the current was pulling me away from them, along the shoreline towards the exposed sandbank. So I swam with it, coughing, spluttering and frantically hoping I could keep going to reach dry land.

I'd never been in such deep water as this, full of powerful forces stirring around me – nothing like calmly swimming a few lengths at the pool. It took all my effort to keep going and not to lose my nerve. By now Uncle Calvin had probably seen where I was heading and would be on his way to drag me onto the sandbank. An image of a seal pup being clubbed to death on a blood-stained beach flashed through my head. Whether it was because of that idea, or just my feeling totally exhausted, I began to give up hope. I stopped swimming, turned on my back to float and catch my breath, then kicked my feet – but I felt myself sinking again and I panicked.

The next few seconds were like something from a Superhero Mega-max movie. Maybe I wasn't meant to die after all. I opened my eyes to see a hand reaching down to pull me from what I assumed were the jaws of death. At first I thought I was seeing things, as I squinted up at a flash of bright yellow and the words 'Surf Rescue' on the lifeguard's jet ski. I had no idea what the lifeguard was saying, but I grabbed his hand and he pulled me up.

The next thing I knew I was being whisked away across the waves while coughing up half the ocean. Holding on to the lifeguard, spluttering astride the jet ski, I watched the pier flash past through the spray as we skimmed over the sea towards the lifeguards' hut and glided to a halt up the beach.

By now I was shivering and my teeth were chattering as I tried to thank my rescuer. I think I said something like he was my knight in shining armour, but as he was only wearing shorts, he didn't seem to understand. He was more interested in all the attention we were getting from everyone on the beach, posing at all the raised phones. He insisted that I went with him up to the lifeguard hut on the promenade for a chat and to fill in a form. That was the last thing I wanted to do, especially as I had to get away fast. It wouldn't take long for Uncle Calvin, the police or anyone else who wanted me locked up to come running.

I sat in the lifeguard's hut with a blanket round my shoulders and sipped something warm and horrible. The other lifeguard on duty was a slim blonde woman in a bright pink bikini. Luckily for me, they were more interested in each other than in keeping a close eye on me. So when their backs were turned, with all their attention on flirting over the paperwork, I slipped out the door and made a run for it. Being barefoot and still feeling a bit wobbly, I knew I'd never outrun them so I had to hide somewhere fast. It was only a short dash across the road to the fairground so, once inside, I could quickly disappear among the crowds. After buying a ticket with a very damp five-pound note, I went in 'The Haunted House', where I could linger in the dark among spiders with flashing red eyes and dancing skeletons. Maybe there were creepy noises too, but this was the least scary part of the day so far. It was safe and I was relieved to be free again. So I snuggled in a corner behind a black curtain and sat as calmly as I could for a very long time – waiting for the coast, and my mind, to clear ...

At the beach hut, after I'd dried out, changed clothes and found new trainers, I was eating a late breakfast of crisps when Sophie arrived, looking serious but with a bit of a sparkle in her eyes. 'I've cracked it,' she began. 'I found what Ella meant by *The Cask Creator*. A quick search took me to Wikipedia and to the word "cooper".'

She showed me what it said on her screen.

> Cooper refers to a profession involved in the work of making utensils, casks, drums and barrels and other accessories, usually out of wood, but may also include other materials.

'So by *The Cask Creator,*' she went on, 'Ella must have meant The Cooper's Inn across the estuary. Mr Rattacheck owns that pub by the cliff tunnel.'

'And it's where Liz Baker is right now,' I said. 'I saw her heading that way. But I reckon that's where Lian could be too – if we're not too late. I've got a terrible feeling she's about to go the same way Ella went two weeks ago tonight. I think there's something about Sundays, but I'm not sure what or where. I've got to find out before the police lock me up as a head case without taking the blindest bit of notice of anything I tell them.'

Sophie touched my hand and said she believed totally in my hunches, then changed the subject by asking how my mum was. That made me feel really bad that I hadn't been able to see her or get in touch.

'Send her a text on my phone,' she said.

While I spelt out a message, I tried to tell Sophie about my fall off the pier and how the police were all over the place looking for me. It was then she showed me the latest on-line news report about me and it made sense why I was public enemy number one.

'But don't worry, I've got you a couple of presents,' she smiled, giving me a carrier bag. 'This year's regatta is all about pirates. There are kids dressed as pirates all over the place. With that headscarf, eye-patch and stripy waistcoat, you'll look like everyone else. We'll need to cross the estuary in the little ferryboat, but dressed like that we stand a better chance. I've also got you a USB recorder stick like Ella's and mine. Seeing as we're on a secret mission ourselves, I thought we'd better have a bit of kit. It's all charged up and ready to go – and so am I!' She handed it to me together with a false beard, but I told her to take hers off as I couldn't lip read if she wore one. It was hard enough to work out what she said in her pirate voice: 'Arrgh, me hearties – now you're a professional undercover investigator disguised as Black Beard. So let's head across the water for a rollickin' spot of a-piratin', a-pillagin' and a-swashbucklin', ah ha.'

The little ferryboat with about twenty passengers sitting around the sides, including a few pirates, nudged onto the beach on the other side of the estuary. Having left her wheelchair in the beach hut, Sophie used her sticks to clamber down a plank, with me supporting her one side and the ferryman the other. I said something about 'walking the plank' in my best pirate voice, but it didn't get a laugh. Maybe I sounded too nervous, as I realised how close we now were to The Cooper's Inn and the scary unknown.

We walked along a beach road towards the cliff, signposted to 'Smuggler's Tunnel leading to Smuggler's Cove'. As we turned a bend, Cooper's Inn came into view, an old stone sea-merchant's house nestling in the rocks, with a veranda full of tables overlooking the estuary, where diners were being harassed by yobby gulls. A sign showed a man making a beer barrel and the words, 'Cooper's Inn: open weekends only. Friday 12.00 – Sunday 22.30'.

I spotted Liz Baker's red sports car at the side of the pub on a gravel drive. Without any idea of what we were going to do, we strolled over to it in the hope we wouldn't be recognised. Sophie pointed below the boot to where the stony ground had been scraped. A line snaked across the drive towards a side door, as if something heavy had been dragged across the gravel and through the door. It looked like a kind of storeroom.

'It could be worth a peep inside,' I said and raised my hand to try the door. Just as I touched the handle, the door swung open and we were confronted by Liz Baker in jeans and scarlet jacket, lips with bright lipstick to match and a cigarette hanging between them.

'What the hell do you want?' she scowled, brushing falling cigarette ash off her jacket. Her eyes were cold and hard, her gelled hair blonder, shorter and spikier than before. The way she stared at me, I knew she could see through my disguise.

'We're looking for Lian,' Sophie said. 'She's a friend of ours.'

'I told you before – she's gone. And good riddance, too.' She blew smoke in my face before grabbing my shirt and pulling me close to her. 'I don't like you, kid. You're trouble and I don't want you anywhere near me. So get out of here and don't let me see you again – or you'll get the biggest surprise of your life.'

I didn't know what to say but tried not to sound scared as she shoved me away from her. 'Are you threatening me again?' I asked.

'Clever boy. You're a fast learner.' She cuffed me round the head and barged past. As soon as she was out of sight round a corner, I turned to Sophie and said, 'Do you see what I mean? She's a nasty piece of work and I'm convinced she killed Ella and I bet she's done something to Lian as well.'

Sophie nodded, 'That threat sounded genuine.'

Even so, I was tempted to try the door in front of us again, now I knew it was unlocked. Once again I raised my hand to turn the handle. Once again the door swung open forcefully. This time a larger figure filled the doorway and a familiar face smiled down at us.

'Ah ha, the pirates have landed,' he smiled.

Mr Rattacheck looked very much like the lord of the manor in his smart white suit, a blue and red checked bowtie and matching shoes. We must have looked like two startled rabbits gawping into the headlights of an approaching juggernaut.

Either Sophie said something funny or extra piratey because he laughed heartily. 'I think I know you two landlubbers. What brings you to my little hideaway on this side of the water?'

I answered with something stupid like, 'We've come to rob your treasure, captain,' which he seemed to think just as funny and shook our hands.

'Then you'd better come inside. Can I tempt you to some coke and a plate of the best chips along this coast? Chef's just sizzled up a fresh batch.'

He led us round to the main entrance then ushered us down steps into a private room with just one table in the middle and a few chairs. An old painting on the wall showed a man bending planks into a barrel, with the title above it: The Cask Creator.

'And how is your charming grandmother, young Sophie?' he asked. 'Will she or anyone be joining us, I wonder?'

He hadn't lost any of his charm and he was a welcome contrast to Liz Baker. I wondered if he realised how nasty she was and why he employed her. It was only when

Sophie told him we weren't with her gran but on our own that I noticed a look in his eyes. Something changed. 'Then why not invite her over, if you like. Give her a call. What time are you being picked up?'

As soon as Sophie took out her phone and said, 'We're going back on our own on the ferry,' he went to the door, slammed it shut then snatched the phone from Sophie's hand.

'You've come snooping, haven't you? I saw you outside on our CCTV. Just like I saw Lian take my boathouse key and hand it to you. I have hidden cameras in all my establishments. You'd be surprised what I've seen. I have drones watching what goes on round here and I've seen more than enough of you two. I knew you were both hiding in my boat when we loaded up the fireworks. I spotted your walking stick in my boathouse. What were you after? What do you want? What did you come here for?'

Although I was shocked by his sudden change, I tried to sound unflustered. 'Nothing.'

He swung round to face me. 'I know all about you. You're in all the papers, you little thug. I could call the police right now and hand you in. For all I know you've come to burn down my business, you little arsonist.'

I took a gamble to see how he'd react. 'You can if you like. I could tell them quite a lot about your business here. I don't need drones to know what's going on. If I tell the police what we found in your boat, that would stop you ever being mayor, wouldn't it?'

'He's right,' Sophie added. 'We know all about Ella. We found something of hers in your boat. It proves her body was in there before she was dumped at sea. We know she was murdered.'

He stared at her, then back to me, then back at Sophie again. 'I've got no idea what you mean. I wouldn't be surprised that whatever it was you found, it was you who planted it there when I generously took you both for a trip. If I'd known this was how you'd repay my kindness, I'd never have taken you. This is absurd. I don't want anything more to do with you.' He turned towards the door. 'One of my staff will come to deal with you in a moment.' He left the room, and suddenly Sophie looked horrified. She signed to me, 'He's locked us in. I heard the key.'

I ran to the door and she was right. We were locked inside the room. When I looked back at Sophie, she signed, 'Don't speak. Sign instead.' She pointed to what looked like a tiny microphone above a window high up the wall. At the other end of the room three steps led down to a small door that was probably to a cellar. I lifted the latch and it opened into a dark corridor. Beckoning Sophie over, I said loudly while pointing at the microphone, 'I think I can climb out the window. I'll pull you up and we can both squeeze through.' Then I signed, 'That should send them looking for us in the other direction.'

I grabbed her hand, pulled her down the steps and closed the door quietly behind us. We were in a long dark passage lit only by a couple of grimy light bulbs. The flaky ceiling and smell of damp was a great contrast to the smart decor and fancy furnishings upstairs. We turned into another passageway and went down more steps. In front of us were three iron doors – only one of which was shut. The others were slightly open, so I gave one a push and peered inside. I expected to see a wine cellar or a room full of barrels, but it looked more like a dungeon. A switch turned on a flickering strip light and immediately the floor became alive with a scurry of glistening cockroaches that quickly disappeared under mattresses set out across the bare room. A pile of blankets was in one corner and a bucket in another. Sophie looked horrified. 'It's like a medieval prison.' The walls and floor were dark brown stone, just like the cliffs. We backed away and I looked at the other door. Although firmly shut, it had a large key in the lock, so I turned it and felt the door clunk open. I pushed it with all my strength, it slowly swung open and I entered the room. It was just like the previous room, except a strip light was already turned on and a dark shape was moving in the corner – something covered with a blanket. As soon as a startled face emerged, we both rushed over to it.

'Lian! Are you okay?'

She squinted at us, looking dazed – until she smiled and threw her arms around us. 'Pirates! However did you get here?'

'We'll tell you later. They'll be coming for us any minute.'

It was high risk to go back the way we'd come, so we went through the third door, which led to more dimly lit passages that twisted and dropped down steps every few metres. We pressed on, with no idea where we were going or if we'd have to go back. Sophie was struggling to keep up and I feared we'd get caught any second. The air was damp and cold now, as if we were deep below ground – then round the next bend we faced another door. Although it was locked, a key hung on a hook in the wall. Cranking open the lock, we pulled the door and entered a wider tunnel running right to left, dropping away steeply but with handrails and brighter lights.

'It's Smuggler's Tunnel,' I said. 'It leads down to the beach through the cliff. I've been down here before when it's been open to the public.'

We headed down the tunnel and soon glimpsed daylight ahead. As we got closer to the end, I could smell seaweed and feel a sea breeze. When we got to the exit, an iron gate barred our way out – padlocked and firmly shut.

'I can't go back,' Sophie groaned.

'There's bound to be someone out there on the beach anytime soon who we can call to for help,' Lian panted. 'In the meantime we can sit here and get our breath back. I've got loads to tell you, so get ready to listen.'

'Thanks,' I grinned. 'Make sure you sit in the light and speak slowly.'

With Lian trying not to gabble and Sophie signing when I got lost, I began to discover just how much danger we were in – right up to our necks.

'Tonight, sometime after midnight, they'll be smuggling people through this tunnel,' Lian began. 'Every

Sunday night Bryn Griffiths brings ashore twenty or more illegal migrants, all desperate people prepared to pay thousands of pounds each to get to Britain. For the next few days they're kept in dreadful conditions in blindfolds or in total darkness in those dungeons, to disorientate them so they can never reveal to anyone where or how they came ashore. Then they're taken by cattle truck to London or the Midlands to slave away in sweatshops. Men, women and children are treated cruelly and threatened while Eros Rattacheck makes a fortune. Ella was about to reveal the whole racket when she was silenced – and the same was about to happen to me. I was told I'd be drowned tonight in a sack full of rocks so I'll never float ashore like poor Ella. They made a mistake with her, as they pushed her off the cliff when the tide was out, which is why Bryn Griffiths had to bury her hours later when it was light – then dump her at sea later, after dark. Their mistake was forgetting Ella's binoculars, which is why Griffiths had to find them – which is when you saw him, Fin.'

'I told you it was Liz Baker who killed her – I knew it,' I said.

'No, she's not the killer. It was Rattacheck himself. He told me he took great pleasure in throwing Ella off the cliff because she knew too much. It was Liz's job to burn all Ella's stuff immediately and get rid of all evidence. Ella must have known Rattacheck was on to her and that he'd kill her if she didn't report him in time. That's why she left that poem.'

She slid a small roll of paper from the hem of her

shorts. 'Since Liz Baker bundled me into her car and drove me here, I've had time to study Ella's final message. Look ... '

She unrolled the poem I'd found in Ella's wallet on the cliff:

Beginning and End

Morning starts the day,
Kissing like a tsunami.
Let the darkness fall ...
Evening stars appear
In the blackest skies,
Ending all our fear ...
Our dreaming never dies.

Ella Brookes

(If you find this
Don't think it must be
A fond farewell end)

Beware the oat crackers!

'At first I thought it was like a haiku,' Lian went on. 'It seemed like Ella just added a few more lines as a kind of goodbye because she knew she was at risk. But it's the title that's the clue. "Beginning and End" means the first and last letters on each line spell out a message.'

By now I was losing the thread of what she was saying, but Sophie looked at the paper closely and spelt it out: 'M, Y, K, I, L, L, E, R, I, S, E, R, O, S.'

'Exactly,' Lian said, 'MY KILLER IS EROS. But then the

next bit says 'Ella Brookes IS DEAD.' She knew she might become his victim. Then there's that bit on the end: "Beware The Oat Crackers." On Twitter she wrote "Beware The Carrot Cakes". Both *The Oat Crackers* and *The Carrot Cakes* are anagrams of Eros Rattacheck. So you see, Ella's last message to the world was a warning about the man who everyone thinks is Mr Wonderful. But he's no more than a people-trafficker and a murderer. I was next on his list of victims, till you managed to rescue me from his clutches.'

It was only when she moved into the light and peered out through the bars of the gate that I saw her black eye. 'Did he do that to you?' I asked.

'And the rest. He was furious that I dared to get a job in his restaurant so I could expose him as a fraud and murderer. He was no more Mister Nice-Guy then, I assure you.'

She flinched when the man himself suddenly appeared behind us, ranting and raving. My heart sank as I knew there was no escape this time. Immediately behind him, men emerged from the darkness of the tunnel. However much we struggled, we were dragged back up the passageway and bundled into the room where we'd found Lian. They threw us on the floor and disappeared, leaving Mr Rattacheck sneering down at us.

'You kids are fools. If you'd waited in the room as I told you, I'd have sent you back home without any fuss. But now I can't. Because of *her* you know too much and I have no choice but to deal with you all accordingly. I am a determined man. And ruthless. Anyone who threatens my ambitions has to be silenced – and pay the price. As soon as it's dark you will be taken from here and disposed of. This time the sea will keep its secrets. No one will know you've drowned, with your bones on the seabed. You'll just be known as "missing". After dark you will be put in a rowing boat and towed out to sea with weights round your necks. Then you'll be scuppered – in other words, a hole punched in the boat and down it goes. What a shame ... a waste of a good boat. But I want you out the way before my next clients silently drift in on the midnight tide.'

We sat stunned as he left the room. I watched Sophie switch off her voice recorder, but we knew it would be no use now. It was over for all of us.

A large moon was rising over the far cliffs and glinting on the sea. Cool wind blew in across the waves that were about to hide more secrets. No one would ever know our fate.

With hands tied behind our backs and in lifejackets filled with sand, we were dragged down steps from the tunnel and into a waiting rowing boat on the beach. Smugglers' Cove was so dark and secluded that shouting for help was pointless, especially with threats that an oar would smack our mouths if any of us 'tried anything stupid'.

As soon as we were thrown into the boat, Liz Baker attached a tow rope to the back of ACE SHOT TRACKER, the speedboat we'd hidden inside only the day before, now bobbing in the breaking waves. She signalled to Mr Rattacheck's henchmen and they pushed our boat into the sea as she started the speedboat's engine. Soon we were bouncing through the night, frightened and frozen from wind and spray. All the time I was trying to work the rope around my wrists loose in the hope of slipping my hands free, but I only succeeded in rubbing my skin raw. Looking behind us, I saw the lights of town and the pier slipping further away. Little had I known earlier that morning as I swam under the pier that I'd be out here hours later, this time sinking to the seabed forever.

The speedboat began to slow, then drift, as Liz Baker pulled on the tow rope to bring us up close. She lit a cigarette and picked up what looked like a harpoon spear, which she tried to ram into our boat. After a few stabs, the wood splintered but held. She swore and said something about 'Plan B', then took a petrol can from the back of the speedboat. Standing on the stern, she began pouring glugs of petrol into our boat around my feet. 'This will warm you up before it sinks in flames,' she laughed, as she untied the rope to cast us adrift. Our boat rose on the swell of a wave and pushed against the speedboat. This was my chance – high risk, I knew. In that instant, I leapt into action. Kicking the back of the speedboat as hard as I could, I hoped to push us far enough away from the match she was about to strike and throw at us. As my foot slammed into her boat, I fell backwards into ours, getting soaked as water and petrol slopped over us. The rest happened so quickly. I had no time to judge how far we were moving apart, when I saw Liz Baker tumble back into her boat from the jolt of my kick. She fell onto the tarpaulin stretched over the back seat, sloshing it with petrol as the can slipped from her grip. The instant her cigarette fell from her mouth, the tarpaulin erupted in a sheet of blue flame that engulfed the back of her boat. Within seconds the fireworks ignited and the entire speedboat burst into a ball of flames and dazzling pyrotechnics. Even though we were drifting away from it, we could feel the heat, and I feared a spark would land in our boat and ignite us as well. Fear kept me wrenching my wrists apart. The rope stretched just enough for me to push my hands down to my feet and, after a lot of wriggling, I slipped my tied hands over my heels and brought them up in front of me. Now I could use my hands for untying Lian and Sophie. Then Lian untied me.

We scrambled around in the boat to get the oars and were soon trying to row away from the fireball just metres away. At the same time we ripped off our heavy 'death-jackets' and hurled them overboard, just as fireworks shot past us and exploded over the sea. But the biggest explosion came a few seconds later when the speedboat's petrol tank went up. The whole boat blew apart in a blinding flash, debris showering over the sea and red smoke belching across the moon.

No one spoke apart from me. 'Blimey – even *I* heard that!' I muttered something about me turning into a full-time arsonist, and stared out over the sea. The blaze died as the boat's smouldering remains sunk below the waves. Cold, wet and smelling of petrol, we kept rowing towards shore in the smoky darkness. The swell of the sea, the wind and currents bounced us around for what seemed forever, before the lights around the estuary eventually drifted nearer and larger. I just hoped Mr Rattacheck wasn't waiting for us on the quay, or that one of his drones was hovering overhead.

Lian was shivering. 'I'm dying for a hot bath, but I guess before that we must let the coastguards know about the next boat sneaking into Smugglers' Cove anytime soon. Then the real fun begins.'

'It's just as well I recorded Rattacheck's outburst,' Sophie said. 'The first thing I'm going to do is take that and our other evidence to the police. You too, Fin?'

I wasn't ready for that yet. I needed a bit more time – time for Mum. I was desperate to contact her before I'd have to spend hours writing statements for the police. So when, at last, we rowed into the harbour and our high-fives were done, all I wanted was to go to the beach hut, put on a jumper, get my stuff and then go to Sophie's gran's to contact Mum on my laptop. But, just like the rest of that Sunday, the night had more surprises of its own.

I lay exhausted in the beach hut, trying to get warm, but finally feeling safe and secure in the stillness. It was a relief to know Lian and Sophie were reporting Rattacheck to the police, but I was concerned about Mum, as I'd received no word from her and she was bound to be worrying about me more than ever. Still with a blanket wrapped around me, I opened the door to look out across the water to where we so nearly drowned. But the water wasn't what I saw. Framed in the doorway, his dimly-lit face staring right at me, stood Uncle Calvin.

I froze, unable to move. I knew I couldn't get past him or run and I had no energy for a fight. My throat tightened, my heart pounded and my stomach heaved. He must have seen the fear in my eyes for he raised a hand and said, 'It's okay.'

I looked around for a weapon but again he said, 'It's okay. I'm not here for trouble. I'm afraid your mother won't make it to the morning. The neighbours lent us their car. We're going over right now if you want to come and say goodbye to her.'

'How did you know I was here?'

'The boy on the pier saw you leave the Haunted House at the fair and followed you. We might just make it to the hospital while she's still conscious. I'm afraid she's only hours from death.'

I think I was too stunned to say anything – or even to cry. I just nodded feebly and followed him to the shiny black Lexus RC F Sport Coupé parked nearby. Jasmine was sitting in the passenger's seat dressed all in black, including gloves. She stared straight ahead, without bothering to look at me when I opened the driver's door, slid the seat forward and climbed through to the cramped back seat.

I stared out through the tinted glass across the water. *If only I'd got in touch with Mum earlier,* I was thinking. I was feeling so numb that I didn't notice Uncle Calvin in the driving seat turning round to talk to me. He shook my knee with his gloved hand. 'I said pass me the keys.'

A key fob was beside me on the back seat, so I handed it to him and he grinned before turning back to start the car. As we sped off towards the cliff road, I watched his eyes in the driver's rear-view mirror. They kept looking at me and I knew he was laughing. It was only then I realised I'd walked into a terrible trap. I caught a smirk on Jasmine's face when she gave Uncle Calvin a smug sideways glance. They weren't taking me to the hospital at all – I was being kidnapped. With no doors or opening windows in the back, I was well and truly trapped. I guessed my best option was to stay calm and pretend I still trusted them. That was easier to think about than to do.

As the car began to slow down, I slipped my hand in my pocket and switched on the USB recorder. My eyes scanned all the lights on the dashboard and saw we were slowing to twenty miles an hour and the time was 23:32. It was almost two weeks to the minute, at this exact spot, where Ella took her last breath. I was still thinking about that when the car steered across the road to a lay-by at the top of the cliff. It was a lay-by that was often full of cars facing the sea, with pensioners sitting with their flasks of tea, admiring the view or dozing. Now it was empty, as the sporty Lexus glided to a stop and Uncle Calvin pulled on the handbrake. He switched on the interior light and spun round to face me. 'Watch my lips,' he grinned. 'It's the end of the road. They all say how clever you are, like your father. But you didn't see this coming, did you? I've outsmarted you this time and at last I've outsmarted him, too.'

'What do you want?' I stuttered. 'Is it still the biscuit tin?'

'There's a bigger prize now. Blame my old man, the mean old git.'

'Don't talk about Grandad like that. He was a better man than you'll ever be.'

I couldn't stop myself shouting back, which made Jasmine spin round and snarl at me. 'What sort of father leaves just five percent of his estate to his only son but the lion's share to a deaf brat of a grandson?'

'The good news is,' Uncle Calvin continued, 'today we sold his flat for two hundred and sixty nine grand. On Tuesday morning I'll be at the solicitors to sort out my rightful inheritance. Instead of my measly five per cent, I shall be getting half your forty-five per cent chunk. And if your mother conveniently passes away in the near future, as expected, I'll get the whole lovely lot. You see, a clause in the old man's will states that if one of us should snuff it before the money is shared out, then the remaining parties divide the deceased's share as well. So it's win-win for Uncle Calvin. First time ever.'

I missed a lot of what he was saying, but I think I got the gist. 'So you've brought me here to get me to sign away my share to you?'

'No need now. You see, you're not as clever as they say.

If I did that, you'd only make a big fuss about it afterwards. No, the plan is simpler. We've brought you here to get rid of you once and for all. It's the best for all of us, seeing as you're no more than a juvenile offender with enough of a criminal record to lock you up for a long stretch. You'd hate that, so we're about to do you and the taxpayer a massive favour, Fin.'

Whether it was the poor light making it tricky to read his lips or because I was scared and exhausted, I just didn't understand what he was saying – although I began to grasp the next bit when he said slowly, 'And now the world will think you've nicked a neighbour's flashy car. Your fingerprints are all over it but ours are nowhere to be found.' They both waved at me with their gloved hands as he continued. 'I got you to pass me the key fob to get your prints on it, even though it's electronic and makes the car work wherever it is inside. It's push-button ignition – and the sort of car I'll be able to afford soon. Unfortunately this particular Lexus is about to smash to bits on the rocks. The police will assume the delinquent of Hillside Road nicked it for an adrenalin-fuelled joyride and sadly skidded off the cliff. Such a shame, but you're bound to get a mention in a touching memorial in your school assembly. I might even give a moving speech about my sad little nephew.'

I took a gamble as I had no idea how he would react. 'Does Jasmine know you've been to prison, Uncle Calvin? Does she know about your violent outbursts called Intermittent Explosive Disorder?'

The awkward look between them told me the answer. He was furious now.

'That was in the past. She doesn't need to know. It was your dad to blame for all that stuff. He was my best mate at school, like the brother I always wanted, before he turned his back on me forever. We planned to travel the world together in our own band. But it was all talk, just so he could get off with my sister. He dumped me to live the life he always wanted. He got the girl, university, money, a kid, success … and I got nothing. That's till tonight. I've got revenge at last – on him, on you and on your grandad. Oh yeah, today I found that biscuit tin in your wardrobe, so now I know you were lying all along. You deserve everything you've got coming … '

He gave Jasmine a nod and she got out of the car, scowling, muttering and slamming the door before going to the front bumper, where she stooped to move boulders from in front of the wheels. The lay-by was edged with small rocks painted white, to stop cars rolling forward over the cliff. He switched off the headlights, released the handbrake, pressed a button to lower his electric window slightly, then pushed the ignition button to close down the dashboard. In the immediate blackness, the only lights I could see were from a couple of blinking buoys far out at sea.

As it dawned on me what they were doing, it was as if my blood had turned to ice and I just couldn't move. My head was spinning and my heart was thumping so fast it felt like it was about to burst. Surely I'd misunderstood him – this couldn't be happening. Even *he* couldn't be this mad. But the next thing I knew, he'd got out, locked both doors automatically from the outside and was posting the fob back in through the narrow gap in the window. Before I had chance to clamber over the passenger seat, I felt the car move as they both pushed from behind. I knew I only had seconds to jump out before the unthinkable happened. The car was rolling forwards as I frantically scrambled into the driver's seat, fumbling in the dark to unlock the door. I couldn't see how to open it and the lock remained firmly shut as I thumped so hard I could feel my fists bleeding and my fingernails tearing as I clawed at the window. The car bumped over the verge of the lay-by … gaining speed as it slid down a grassy slope towards the cliff edge. With both hands, I yanked at the handbrake. The car slowed but still my fingers couldn't find a catch to release the door – as the handbrake juddered and the wheels continued to bump over ruts. I grabbed the steering wheel to turn the car off course, but it wouldn't budge – the steering lock was rigid. My feet tried to find the footbrake, but in the mad panic I forgot which pedal it was. I'd driven Mum's car out of the garage before, but I just couldn't remember which pedal was which – so I slammed my feet down on all of them, praying one would stop the car as it trundled on. It was the middle one that slowed the wheels, so I kept my foot jammed on it, even though I knew I wouldn't be able to hold it there for long. But what if …

I thumped the ignition button, the dashboard flashed into life and the steering wheel unlocked instantly.

Fumbling at where I thought the headlight switch was, I flicked at it and the night lit up – the grass falling away in front of me to oblivion just beyond. It was a mad thought, but now I'd worked out which pedal was the clutch, I pushed my other foot down on it, grabbed for the gearstick, pushed it and lifted up both feet. The car juddered, jolted and leapt forward as I wrenched the steering wheel round to the right. Immediately the car swerved and skidded up the grass bank, then slowed as the wheels spun in the mud – but there was power in those wheels as I pushed my foot hard on the accelerator pedal and felt the car pulling upwards – back towards the lay-by.

Scared rigid that I'd stall the engine and roll backwards, I kept my foot on the accelerator and ensured the handbrake was off – just as I hit one of the boulders at the edge of the lay-by. The car smashed over it, tipping violently to one side before bouncing onto tarmac, where I glimpsed Uncle Calvin in the headlights, looking horrified as I sped towards him. He picked up a large stone and hurled it at me. The windscreen cracked as I swerved past him and steered onto the road, heading downhill towards town. Desperate to get away, I drove in the middle of the road, hardly able to see where I was going through the shattered windscreen. I slipped the car out of gear, hoping to roll gently down to town, with only the footbrake and steering to worry about.

Just as I turned a bend, I saw headlights coming up the hill towards me. Unable to see markings on the road, I couldn't judge how much room I had to pass the oncoming car. I pulled over to the left but clipped the edge of the road, which sent me swerving into the middle. Then I saw it was a police car in my headlights. We flashed past each other with just a centimetre between us, but our wing mirrors hit and flew off, just as I caught sight of the driver shouting at me. I didn't stop, but let the Lexus keep rolling downhill while I looked in the rear-view mirror to see the police car stopping and about to turn round. The last thing I wanted was a car chase through town, so I turned off along the seafront and began to slow down. I switched off the headlights and turned into a car park, but could no longer see a thing. The car slowed but suddenly hit something – the airbags going off in my face.

I sat stunned for a few seconds before switching off the ignition and trying to open the door. It was impossible to unlock, and in my desperation to get away, I raised my feet over the dashboard and slammed them into the windscreen, which instantly burst in a shower of tiny fragments. Climbing out through the hole, I slid across the bonnet over all the broken glass and stood looking back at the dented Lexus with a smashed headlight, where it had hit the corner of the lifeboat station. Only then I realised I'd cut my hand on a jagged edge as the blood trickled through my fingers.

It wasn't far from there to the beach hut, so I ran to the nearest steps down to the beach, where I stood alone and very still in the shadows before walking along the water's edge towards the harbour. Looking across the estuary to where the Cooper's Inn was in pitch darkness, I felt as if I was the only person left on the planet. Not a soul was about and for the first time for days I felt strangely calm. In that solitude, just after midnight, the vast sky appeared unusually clear, sprinkled with stunning starlight. Despite everything, it suddenly felt great to be alive – particularly as I wasn't meant to be.

Instead of hiding away in the beach hut, I wanted to savour the tranquil scene around me, so I sat on the sand and stared at the moon reflected in the water. The wind had now dropped, the quayside was deserted and the night was very still. With my fingers still bleeding and a hanky tied around my hand, I lay back, looked up at the stars, as if Mum was somewhere in the midnight sky, and I spoke to her. 'Sorry. I'm sorry for everything. I love you, Mum. Always.'

In that moment, as if she was answering from the heavens, the moon seemed to turn blue – sparking across the dark water and sweeping over moored yachts swaying gently in a wisp of shimmering mist. Shiny wet shingle on the beach flashed around me and my head pounded with pulsing light. Only when I turned to look behind me did I realise a police car was skidding to a halt on the quayside. It was like watching a silent movie in slow motion … flickering and juddering; unreal, like a dream from another world.

I calmly stood to face the policemen and dogs running across the shingle towards me, silhouetted against the headlights and swirling blue light. I guess there was a lot of shouting and barking, as truncheons rose and handcuffs clamped on my wrists.

'It's okay,' I said quietly. 'I'm Fin. You don't have to use all that stuff. I'm not a bad kid. Mum would've told you that. Grandad would be so proud of me.'

They gripped my arm, forced it behind my back and led me up the beach to the waiting car.

EIGHTEEN

December

They say it's not over till the fat lady sings. In that case, she probably hasn't even got out of bed yet. If the fat lady is Jasmine, she won't be singing for a long time. She and Uncle Calvin have been charged with stealing a car and attempted murder – amongst other things. I'll be asked to give evidence at their court case sometime next year. Sophie, Lian and I will also have to attend Ella's murder trial. Mr Rattacheck has been charged with her murder, as well as with attempted murder (of us). He and Bryn Griffiths are also charged with all kinds of people-trafficking, immigration offences and kidnapping, so I'm going to get used to being in courtrooms with my own personal signer. We've been told it could all go on for a long time.

Of all the things Uncle Calvin did to me, I think the worst was his lie that Mum was about to die that night. I knew she was seriously ill, but I'm so angry I believed him. Even though she's still in hospital and I go to see her twice a week, she was never only 'hours from death'. I can't forgive him for that. I genuinely thought I'd never see her again, and it was a long time before anyone on the youth offenders team told me she was still alive. The worst hours of my life were just after my arrest when I felt so alone and no one believed what I was telling them. The frustrating thing was – I was the deaf one, yet I was the one no one was listening to. If it weren't for Mrs Homes coming to my rescue, I'd have gone mad.

However much I told them what happened, very few adults believed me at first. I don't think they liked hearing the truth. They were convinced I'd stolen the Lexus from next door. Nobody wanted to listen to what we had to say – probably because Sophie and I were 'just kids' and 'disabled'. Nobody wanted to listen to Lian because she was an 'outsider', from another race. And maybe, if Ella had been a male journalist, she may never have been a victim. I've learned how prejudice can deafen people who reckon they can hear perfectly. Sometimes there are none so deaf as those who will not hear.

I've only been back home to our bungalow once. My police worker took me there so I could collect a lot of my stuff – and to return Grandad's biscuit tin to my wardrobe. I now live with Mrs Holmes most of the time. Sometimes I stay at Mrs Boughtwood's and help with the animals. Although I've got used to being 'of no fixed abode', I so want to live with Mum again. Just the two of us. We've got our fingers crossed they'll let her home for Christmas. That would be awesome.

I haven't told Mum everything about what happened. Not yet. She's already had enough set-backs. I haven't asked her about my dad yet, either. The other day I googled his name. He's a professor of veterinary medicine in the United States, which I reckon is really cool.

The hospital didn't want to take my stem cells for ages, but in the end it was Mum's only hope. I was the youngest donor they'd ever had. We finally got the green light a few weeks ago. I went to the hospital all day for what they call the 'harvesting' and my cells were then frozen because she wasn't well enough to receive them at the time. Her leukaemia cells kept coming back, so she had to have more and stronger chemo till they were all properly zapped.

It was a relief to get the message telling me I could finally go to the hospital to give blood. I had appointments with the transplant nurse and doctors, who made Mum sign lots of forms, then tested my blood yet again for viruses and stuff. Then I had injections for four days to boost my stem cells. Eventually I was taken to the Apheresis Unit, which is where they do what is called Peripheral Blood Stem Cell Harvesting. I had to lie on a bed for five hours after they put a tube called a cannula in both my arms. It didn't hurt because they rubbed on an anaesthetic cream. Then I was connected to the Apheresis machine – which took blood from one arm, whizzed it around to collect my cells in a bag, then sent the blood back into my other arm. Every so often a nurse would check my blood pressure, pulse and temperature and I found it all really interesting. I think I could be a doctor as well as a vet.

When I was disconnected at last and my stem cells were collected by the lab staff, I had to wait another hour to see if I'd given enough cells or whether I'd have to return the next day. Yay! I'd given enough!

A couple of weeks ago Mum got the all-clear that she could be given my three little bags of stem cells. I told them to make sure they defrosted them all properly, as I knew what it's like for blood to run cold (like whenever I think of Uncle Calvin!)

So now we must wait for what's called 'engraftment', when my cells make their way to Mum's bone marrow where they should hopefully grow and mature into normal blood cells. That can take several weeks, but so far her blood count is slowly picking up, although her immune system is still zilch. I just hope this will save her life. It's been a tough time for her – and, to be honest, I've struggled a bit, too.

It hasn't been easy being fourteen so far. Sophie, her gran and Mrs Holmes have been amazing at keeping me together. They've been brilliant and nagged me to write all this down in my own words without giving up. They added a few bits of their own to the parts they remembered

– to jog me along. Mrs Holmes helped with punctuation and grammar, and suggested vocabulary or similes (she's got a thing about adjectives and descriptions). She typed up all the conversations from the USB recording sticks word for word, once the police had taken copies for evidence. So I wrote all this for them, as much as for me. I'm going to dedicate it to Grandad and give a copy to Mum when she comes home. I bet she'll cry, especially when I tell her how the Fin she once knew is now someone quite different.

I often think about the Fin I used to be, innocently balancing stones on a sunny beach in August. I'm not too sure about the Fin I've become, or how all this will end, if it ever will. I'm not sure of anything anymore – apart from how so much changed in one short summer. I certainly can't be sure what things will be like next summer, let alone what the next chapter might bring.

They still want me to have cochlea implants, as though that's the answer to unlocking my future, breaking the silence and solving everything. I'm just not certain. I'd like to believe in happy endings, but I reckon, like tooth fairies, they stay hidden, disguised as something else – or are just a figment of the imagination. Whatever happens, whether I ever break the silence completely, make sense of everything or try to build up again the pieces from that summer, I can only hope from now on I manage to get the balance right.

I guess that means 'taking things steady' as Mum puts it. I've got a feeling my balancing act could last a while …

maybe a lifetime. Then again, living the next chapter, like turning a new page, might be no bigger deal than simply trying to balance the next stone. And that happens to be just up my street.

Dedication:

To Bren – whose brave and long journey with MDS has inspired us all.

www.mdspatientsupport.org.uk
anthonynolan.org
www.dkms.org.uk/en

John Townsend was born in Chelmsford, Essex, and discovered his enchantment with books at an early age. As a child, he wrote mini-dramas, silly poems and stories to tell the cat. Whether or not the cat wanted to hear them is another matter!

His love of hiking and the outdoors led him to become a geography teacher in Gloucestershire, writing pantomimes and plays for the annual drama productions. His first publication was inspired by his rusty old Morris Minor and, 200 books later, he is now a full-time writer.